D0273673

. . . and Her Amazing Clones

'Angela Woolfe has created a winning formula, combining comic characters, true friendship and a pacy plot with, at times, a very real sense of menace. More please!'

Philip Ardagh

Edinburgh City Libraries **Nt**	
C002807922 1	
Askews	26-Mar-2008
DIP	£4.99

AVRIL CRUMP

. . . and Her Amazing Clones

Angela Woolfe

EGMONT

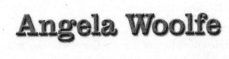

For my parents, Helen and Stephen,
and for Josh.
With love and thanks.

Published in Great Britain 2004
by Egmont Books Limited
239 Kensington High Street, London W8 6SA

Text copyright © 2004 Angela Woolfe
Cover and illustrations copyright © 2004 Oliver Burston

The moral rights of the author and illustrator have been asserted

ISBN 1 4052 0747 7

5 7 9 10 8 6 4

A CIP catalogue record for this title is available from the British Library

Typeset by Avon DataSet Ltd, Bidford on Avon
Printed and bound in Great Britain by the CPI Group

This paperback is sold subject to the condition that it shall not, by way of trade or otherwise, be lent, resold, hired out, or otherwise circulated without the publisher's prior consent in any form of binding or cover other than that in which it is published and without a similar condition including this condition being imposed on the subsequent purchaser.

Contents

THE WRETCHFORD POST

Your indispensable weekly source of news, views and movie reviews for Wretchford-on-the-Reeke and the surrounding area.

LABORATORY TO RE-OPEN

Local history will be made today when Leviticus Laboratories opens its gates to the public for the first time in fifteen years.

The renowned scientific institution has not admitted visitors since the well-known human-cloning scandal fifteen years ago. Professor Gideon Blut, the scientist responsible, was expelled after malformed cloned body parts were found in his office. Blut, who was allegedly trying to create a super-clone from the cells of famous historical figures, was charged by the Governors with conducting an Unauthorised Experiment. He disappeared in mysterious circumstances. Police are still interested in determining his whereabouts.

Professor Schnauzbart, Head of the Oil and Fuel Department and Chief Governor at Leviticus, will hope this black mark is forgotten today when he leads a party of local bigwigs and journalists on a tour around the Laboratories. They will be shown interesting experiments and listen to a short lecture before enjoying sherry and nibbles in the staffroom. It is expected that regular tours will follow over the next few months.

1

Leviticus

The small crowd pressed wind-chilled faces against the tall iron gates, pushing and shoving for a glimpse through the bars. A thick red carpet was being unrolled from the grand oak doorway; the brass lettering on the sign above the entrance was being buffed to a high shine; a gaggle of gossiping cleaners leaned on idle brooms, complaining about their aching backs and drinking mugs of tea.

The gates began to creak open.

'Ladies and gentlemen, welcome to Leviticus!'

The small group of visitors gazed in awe at the man who had spoken. He cut an imposing figure in his crisp white labcoat, his dark hair shining in the chill winter sunlight, his rather large nose flaring with pride and excitement.

'I, Dr Wetherby, Deputy Head of the Oil and Fuel Department and Director of Experimental Affairs, feel deeply honoured to show such a distinguished group of visitors the wonders of . . .'

He stopped. He stared at the tour party. Twenty grubby faces stared back. They did not look distinguished at all. They looked extremely *un*distinguished. Positively mediocre, in fact.

'Where's the mayor?' Dr Wetherby hissed. 'Where are the TV reporters? Who are *you* lot?'

A spotty youth in a pom-pom hat stepped forward.

'We're from the campsite down the road,' he offered. 'They said they needed people for a rehearsal of this tour you're doing later.'

Dr Wetherby reached into his pocket for his schedule. He glowered at the piece of paper and squinted to read the small print he had not noticed earlier: *1 p.m.*, it read, *practice run of tour – led by Dr Wetherby*. This was followed underneath by even smaller print: *2 p.m. actual tour – led by Professor Schnauzbart*. Grinding his teeth, Dr Wetherby ripped the schedule into tiny shreds before taking all seventeen pages of his big speech and doing the same. He made a mental note to fire his secretary.

The spotty youth's face glowed with excitement.

'Oh, and we were promised sherry and nibbles. Don't suppose we could have those first?'

'Right,' Dr Wetherby snapped, casting the shreds of paper to the wind. 'Let's get this over with.'

He stamped off towards the main building, shoving the tea-slurping cleaners out of his way.

'Get a move on!'

The campers hurried after him as he led them past the magnificent oak doors and around to the side entrance. Dr Wetherby did not want any of his colleagues seeing him leading the warm-up tour. Purple-faced and furious, he swept the motley party through endless grey corridors at high speed.

'That's a laboratory.' He gestured into empty rooms as they sped along. 'That's another one . . . toilets . . . stationery cupboard . . . another lab . . .'

'What happened in *there*?' piped up the woolly-hatted youth, rather out of breath, pointing back at the burnt-out laboratory they had just passed.

'Oh, one of my junior colleagues blew several labs up a couple of weeks ago,' Dr Wetherby replied, scurrying past the row of smoke-blackened doors and peering around a corner before ushering his group down yet another corridor. He glanced at his watch. Three minutes twenty-four seconds was long enough for a tour, wasn't it?

'Well,' he said, 'this has been a great privilege for you. Now please leave immediately.' He shooed them with a dismissive hand. 'Back to your campsite.'

There was a mutinous rumbling from the group.

'They said sherry and nibbles . . . Not so much as a fried-egg sarnie . . . Wouldn't hurt them to give us a drink . . .'

'Now, look . . .' Dr Wetherby began. But before he could continue, a glamorous young woman with long, smooth, dark hair and large sunglasses came into view at the end of the corridor and began sashaying towards them.

Dr Wetherby's heart stopped.

'In here!' he gasped, shoving several unhappy campers at a time through the nearest laboratory door. He pressed his back firmly against it and prayed that Dr Sedukta, of all people, hadn't seen him. 'There are nibbles in here,' he lied, 'but you must be *very* quiet . . .'

He was scanning the large, empty laboratory for somewhere he might be able to hide in case Dr Sedukta followed them when his eye lit upon a door at one side of the room. It was labelled Chemical Store Cupboard.

'Hey, there are no nibbles in here . . .'

But Dr Wetherby was ignoring the campers. To his consternation, what looked like steam had suddenly begun to emerge from beneath the Chemical Store Cupboard door. He blinked, hoping his eyes were playing tricks on him, but the trail of steam continued. There couldn't be *another* explosion, not while there were visitors around!

The cupboard door creaked open. Slowly, uncertainly, a small chubby hand began to appear, followed by a large chubby head. The head was almost completely bald, the face beneath it round, smooth and rather pink.

'Hello,' it said nervously.

The entire tour party stopped grumbling and stared in amazement. The newcomer's appearance was strange enough, but the voice was even more peculiar. It swooped and plummeted between a high squeak and a deep boom.

Dr Wetherby felt faint. 'Dr Crump! I might have known!'

'I wasn't expecting to see you, Dr Wetherby,' the balding figure squeaked.

'So I see, Avril.' Dr Wetherby made meticulous use of his juniors' first names whenever he wanted to make them appear childish and foolish. 'According to Rule seventeen, Paragraph twelve, Subsection three of the Leviticus Manual for Laboratory Technicians, only authorised personnel are permitted to enter the store cupboards. So tell me, what *are* you doing lurking around in there?'

'I'm just at the critical stage of a . . . er . . . a rather important experiment . . .'

Steam continued to billow from behind the door, accompanied now by a low bubbling sound.

Dr Wetherby's thick eyebrows shot upwards in alarm as he took several hasty paces backwards. 'It isn't going to *explode*, is it?'

'No,' Avril boomed. 'It's really nothing at all!'

'You said it was an *important experiment*.' Dr Wetherby pointed an accusing finger, though he did not move any closer. 'Given your track record, Avril, and last month's Official Warning for blowing up four of my lovely laboratories, you will forgive me for being a little suspicious. Tell me the truth: are you concocting another of your ridiculous mops in there?'

'They're not mops,' Dr Crump protested. 'They're *sponges*. But I'm not doing anything like that, Dr Wetherby. I promised Professor Schnauzbart I'd only do it in my own time from now on . . .'

'But Professor Schnauzbart doesn't want you to do it *at all*, Avril! And neither do I! It's all very well trying to create some ludicrous giant sponge to clear up oil spills, but the real environmental hazard is your explosions on land . . .'

In mid-sentence, he heard the door click open behind him and he spun round in a panic.

'Dr Sedukta,' he said. 'How nice to see you.'

'Likewise,' said Dr Sedukta, sliding a hand into the pocket of her designer labcoat. Her teeth were very white against deep red lips and, despite the bright electric lighting, she was wearing her customary dark sunglasses, which gave her an even more exotic air. 'I saw you out in the corridor and wondered what fun I was missing.' She gazed around at the gathering. 'Is this a private party, or can anyone join in?'

'Not much of a party without nibbles,' came a loud voice from the crowd, which was beginning to grow restless.

Dr Wetherby was now puce with embarrassment. He decided to divert attention by picking on Avril Crump instead.

'I am glad you came in, Dr Sedukta,' he said. 'I shall need a witness to this. Avril Crump appears to be conducting a secret experiment in the cupboard, an experiment for which she has not asked my permission.'

Dr Sedukta shook her head disapprovingly. 'And so soon after those explosions,' she drawled. 'April and her mops! She really is quite the maverick!' She moved closer to Dr Wetherby and coyly twirled a silver ring on her right hand.

Dr Crump sighed. Dr Sedukta had been at Leviticus for nearly a month now, and she still kept getting her name wrong.

'It's Avril. And it's *sponges*. And those explosions weren't *completely* my fault. I told the Governors there was just a little mistake in my polypropylene. And this is nothing to do with sponges, really it isn't . . .'

But Dr Wetherby was on a roll. 'I am your boss, Avril,' he reminded her, waving away a swirl of steam. 'You had better tell me exactly what you are up to in there, or I shall presume it to be an *Unauthorised Experiment*!'

'Go and look at it!' Dr Sedukta suddenly hissed, poking Wetherby in the ribs with a long fingernail. 'See what she's doing in there!'

'Yeah!' said the woolly-hatted camper, poking Wetherby in the ribs with a filthy fingernail. 'Go and see! You're in charge around here, aren't you?'

'Go on!' the crowd joined in. 'Don't be a wimp, mate . . . What are you, a man or a mouse?'

Dr Wetherby groaned inwardly. He could not seem like a coward in front of Dr Sedukta.

'Go on then, fatso, move!' he snarled at Dr Crump, flinging the door wide open. He swiped at the steam that rushed out before it was clear enough to take a step inside.

At the back of the cupboard, there was a low table. Resting on its rickety surface was a small black pot perched on a stand, heated by the flame of a single Bunsen burner.

Dr Wetherby took a step towards the pot. It certainly didn't look like one of Dr Crump's spongy materials in there. Was it a dangerous acid, a hazardous alkali, some lethal cocktail of highly explosive fossil fuels? Hardly daring to breathe, Dr Wetherby leaned over and peered gingerly into the pot.

'*Baked beans?*'

He whirled around.

'Heating up a *can of beans*? And still *in* the can too! What sort of Unauthorised Experiment is *that*?'

'It's not an Unauthorised Experiment,' Dr Crump squeaked. 'It's lunch.'

'Well, it's an Unauthorised Lunch!' Dr Wetherby

roared, storming out of the cupboard as Dr Sedukta and the tour group began howling with laughter. 'What's the matter with you, girl?' he hissed at Dr Crump. 'Can't you eat in the canteen like everyone else?'

'I do,' she protested, 'but it's cauliflower surprise today. That's not a proper lunch. I'm a growing woman!'

'Growing *outwards*, unfortunately,' Dr Wetherby sneered down at her, 'not *upwards*.'

'Well, it's no fried-egg sandwich, but any port in a storm. That's camper grub, that is,' declared the woolly-hatted youth.

Dr Wetherby marched across to Dr Sedukta as Avril fought off hungry campers. 'I think we've seen enough here,' he said through clenched teeth. 'Shall we go and have *our* lunch in the canteen?' He grasped her elbow and began to hustle her from the room. 'And you lot – get out before I call Security!' he hissed at the campers, turning back briefly to glower at Avril. He would deal with her later.

'Hey!' called the woolly-hatted camper, diverted from his fight for baked beans. 'They've got a canteen! I can taste that cauliflower surprise already. Follow me, boys!'

Dr Crump sighed with relief as the door slammed

shut behind the departing tour party, leaving her standing alone beside the bubbling baked bean pot. She fished a slightly grubby spoon from the deep pocket of her labcoat and tucked in.

Nobody knew how old Avril Crump was, although her nearly bald head and smooth, round, pink face made her look like a cheerful, overgrown baby. Being round, pink and bald had been fine when she actually *was* a baby, but it had caused her problems from the moment she had stopped being a baby and started nursery school. Despite her cheery demeanour and generosity with her toys, she was so strange-looking that the children left her entirely alone. Every day, little Avril would sit in a corner with her train set, wondering who she might be able to talk to over milk and biscuits at break time. But break time would come and go, and nobody would even smile at her, however brightly she beamed, and however many times she offered up her own biscuits as a consolation prize for whoever drew the short straw and had to sit next to her.

Things were even worse when Avril started at the village school in her childhood home of Bleeksby-on-Sea. Not only did the children here have hair, they also had fingers that pinched and fists that pummelled and shrill, mean little laughs. The girls in her class formed the Avril Crump's a Bald Fat Lump Society, leaning across her in the classroom to hiss the day's secret password at each other. By the second week of school, Avril had given up offering her biscuits around in exchange for friendship. There was not a single taker. She pretended not to notice the whispers and sniggers that followed her wherever she went, but some of them seeped through: '*Who's the fat freak?*' . . . '*Watch out for your lunch, Crumpy's coming*' . . . '*Avril Crump's a bald, fat lump, Avril Crump's a bald, fat lump*' . . .

Avril tried not to let this get to her. She taught herself to read proper books, so that her break times could at least be filled with stories. She saved up her small amount of pocket money and bought paper and crayons, so that she could occupy her time drawing pictures during the long school holidays when all the other children were out in the streets, playing with their friends. She developed an interest in collecting insects, as they were the only living creatures that didn't run away from her, and spent hour after hour making homes for them from old matchboxes. But every night, in her bed, the darkness set free the thoughts that the daylight would not allow, and Avril would find herself sniffing away the tears and longing for something that would make her happy.

Luckily for pink, bald, friendless little Avril, she did not have too long to wait.

It all began with Auntie Primula on Avril's sixth birthday. The tea party had been doomed to disaster from the start, as Avril had not handed out the invitations her mother had written. There was no one to give them to. The pretty pink cards had become glued together in her coat pocket with melted chocolate and half a dead spider she had been meaning to bury.

So it was that young Avril sat alone on her birthday at a tea table straining under the weight of fairy cakes and chocolate ice cream. Dirty Julian from down in the village, who shared Avril's insect craze, had originally offered to come, but they had fallen out over a giant ladybird the previous week, and they were still not talking to each other. In the kitchen of the Crumps' little cottage, Avril's mother sobbed and waved a nasty-looking bread knife. In the dining room, Avril ate a fifth doughnut while lifting up the corners of the sandwiches. She looked around at the empty seats and tried very hard not to mind that there would be no one to share her birthday cake with. This was not shaping up to be the world's best ever sixth birthday.

Then the doorbell rang.

'Oh!' gasped Avril's mother, running through the dining room to get to the front door. 'That must be a guest! How brave – er – how *lovely*!' she corrected herself, as Avril lowered her bald head in humiliation. 'I'll go and let them in.'

Who could have known about her birthday party? Avril listened anxiously to the muffled voices coming from the hallway as she slipped an emergency doughnut up her sleeve. She was desperate to share her cake, but she didn't fancy the doughnuts going to the members of the Avril Crump's a Bald Fat Lump Society. Although it didn't sound like *any* of her classmates. It didn't even sound like Dirty Julian, who sniffed three times a sentence. Then Avril heard her mother wail, followed by her footsteps running up the stairs. Perhaps it *was* Dirty Julian after all.

The dining-room door opened. A powerful aroma of cat wafted – no, *surged* – through the air, knocking even robust little Avril off her chair.

'Hello, Auntie Primula,' she said as she got to her feet.

'HAPPY BIRTHDAY, YOUNG LADY!' Auntie Primula may have smelled like a cat, but she sounded like a herd of stampeding rhinos. She was wearing her usual uniform of a tweed deerstalker hat and a skirt like a circus tent.

Avril clamped a thumb and forefinger over her nose. 'Thank you, Auntie Primula,' she said politely.

Auntie Primula was fond of little Avril, regarding her as something of a kindred spirit.

'NO GUESTS, EH? WELL, I ALWAYS SAY GUESTS RUIN A GOOD PARTY. AH, IS THAT A SPARE DOUGHNUT?' She reached down an enormous hand and snatched the stray emergency doughnut that had just fallen out of Avril's sleeve.

'DELICIOUS,' she munched. Red jam oozed down her chin.

'Auntie Primula, would you like a glass of lemonade?' Avril asked.

'CAN'T, I'M AFRAID, YOUNG LADY. IN A BIT OF A HURRY. JUST CAME TO DROP OFF YOUR PRESENT.'

'Oh.' Avril's heart sank. On her fourth birthday, Auntie Primula had given her a framed photograph of a dead cat. On her fifth birthday, Auntie Primula had given her a stuffed cat – not a cute, cuddly, toy-shop stuffed cat; a real, *dead* stuffed cat that had been kept in the freezer for months. She could hardly bear to imagine what feline horror was in store for her today. 'That's . . . kind of you, Auntie Primula.'

'NOT A BIT OF IT. NOW, WHERE DID I PUT IT?' She began rummaging through her colossal brown handbag. 'GOLLY, I WONDERED WHERE THAT WAS . . . EXCELLENT. I KNEW MY FALSE TEETH WOULD SHOW UP SOONER OR LATER . . . AH, BETTER THROW *THAT* OUT SHARPISH, I THINK . . . NOW, HERE WE ARE . . .' She pulled out a large wooden box. 'HAPPY BIRTHDAY.'

Avril gulped as she took the box. It looked just the right sort of size for a cat. In fact, it looked rather like a cat's coffin. Her podgy hands trembled.

'WELL, AREN'T YOU GOING TO OPEN IT?'

Avril knelt down to stop her knees from shaking and placed the box on the floor. She closed her eyes very tightly. Dead insects were one thing; dead pets quite another. She prepared herself for the worst and lifted the lid.

'UNCLE EDGAR'S CHEMISTRY SET? HOW DID *THAT* GET IN THERE? WHERE ARE THOSE SWEET LITTLE KITTENS?'

'C-chemistry set?' squeaked Avril, opening one eye. She looked into the box. It was filled with strange and exciting objects – glass tubes and metal dishes. She reached underneath the top layer. There lay packets of brightly coloured powders and vials of jewel-coloured liquids.

'NOW, LET ME THINK. I GOT THE SHOP TO STUFF THOSE KITTENS YESTERDAY, AND I DEFINITELY BROUGHT THEM HOME. I MUST HAVE MUDDLED UP THE BOXES.' Auntie Primula was red-faced.

'But Auntie Primula, this is a *wonderful* present!' Avril's eyes shone as she picked her way through the marvels of the box. 'It's the best present I've ever had.'

'ALL VERY WELL, BUT HOW AM *I* GOING TO FIND ROOM FOR TWO MORE STUFFED KITTENS? PEOPLE WILL START TO THINK I'M WEIRD.' Auntie Primula zipped up her handbag and stomped to the door. 'KEEP THE CHEMISTRY SET IF YOU REALLY WANT. HEAVEN KNOWS, IT DID POOR UNCLE EDGAR NO GOOD. HE'D PROBABLY STILL BE ALIVE TODAY IF IT HADN'T BEEN FOR THAT UNFORTUNATE EXPLOSION.' She galumphed into the hallway. 'ENJOY THE PARTY, YOUNG LADY!'

And she was gone, though the smell remained.

Avril ran her hand along the smooth, dark wooden

lid, feeling a thrill weave its way through her body from top to toe. She abandoned the laden tea table, doughnuts and all, gathered up the heavy box and made her way upstairs to her room. She placed the box on her little desk and sat down in front of it. *Cobalt chloride* . . . *Sodium bicarbonate* . . . the packets whispered to her as she lifted them to read the names . . . *Ammonium sulphate* . . . *Tannic acid* . . . The sniggers and taunts Avril longed to forget were drowned out of her head. She had found it. She had found the thing that would make her happy.

From that day on, Avril's life was devoted to experimenting. She never noticed the funny looks and didn't care that she had no friends. Her head was too full of the wonders of scientific possibility. At school, she failed in every subject but Chemistry, Physics and Biology, in which she got top marks. At university, she astounded fellow students with her brilliant research into the possibilities of harnessing wave power for energy. The Crump Oscillating Water Column had won prizes for its ground-breaking design, though its liability to slowly rust in sea water meant that it had never been used in practice. And now here she was, working at the once world-famous Leviticus Laboratories, the pinnacle of any scientist's career.

* * *

'I *hate* Dr Wetherby,' she muttered through a mouthful of piping-hot baked beans. 'He's always putting me down. Just because *he* thinks it's a crime to need a second lunch.'

Dr Wetherby had been Avril's boss ever since she had arrived at Leviticus nearly three years ago. He had never been exactly nice to her, but his insults had worsened since the arrival of Dr Sedukta, keen as he was to impress her. Worse than his rudeness, however, far worse, was his lack of scientific curiosity. He was a real stick-in-the-mud, refusing to listen to any ideas Avril put to him, and ignoring all her suggestions for exciting new experiments.

Working in the prestigious Oil and Fuel Department should have been a dream come true for Avril. Ever since she had seen at first hand the havoc wrought by a massive oil spill just off the Bleeksby coast when she was twelve years old, she had wanted to use science to create new, harmless sources of fuel. Her Crump Oscillating Water Column was just one of her many innovations. Avril had also tried extracting the geothermal energy from hot, dry rocks, and attempted to harness the power of the sun to drive everything from tractors to jet engines. But since taking up her latest job, Avril's enthusiasm had begun to drain away.

Professor Blut and his human-cloning scandal had done far more damage to Leviticus Laboratories than simply dragging its good name through the dirt. Fearful of pushing the boundaries too far, no one at Leviticus had dared try anything new for the last fifteen years. Eventually, Avril had given up trying to persuade them to begin work on an alternative fuel source, and decided instead to work on the matter of clearing up environmental disasters. She had read about new techniques of creating genetically modified bacteria to eat up spilled oil, but thought that sounded rather cruel. She had heard about chemical dispersants, which would break up oil and dilute it into the water, but these could not be used without harming nearby wildlife. Avril was on the hunt for something different. One day, lying in the bath and playing with her rubber ducks and sponge, Avril had had a brainwave. Leaping out of the bath like Archimedes, she had begun to scribble down jottings and chemical formulae for a giant, super-absorbent sponge, so powerful that it could suck up vast areas of spilled oil within minutes.

Months later, she was still experimenting. So far,

none of her artificial sponge materials had been absorbent enough, but that hadn't stopped her. All right, so she had accidentally blown up four labs in the process, but that was only because she was trying to achieve something ground-breaking and world-changing, instead of producing one measly graph or half a useless formula like the other 458 Leviticus scientists, in all departments, were content to do year after year.

Avril scraped the last of the beans from the little pot. '*Growing outwards, unfortunately, not upwards* . . .' she said aloud, doing her very best impersonation of Dr Wetherby. Well, he could sneer at someone else in future. She had had enough. She was resigning. She was getting out of here, and she would conduct her sponge experiments in private from now on.

Tootling off down the quiet corridor towards her secret hideaway, where she could write her resignation letter in peace and quiet, Avril was heedless of the sharp pair of eyes watching her from behind large sunglasses, heedless of the hushed voice whispering into a mobile phone.

'Sedukta here . . . yes, I know I haven't reported anything interesting yet, but nothing interesting ever happens around here . . . Look, you know you told me to look out for mavericks at Leviticus, people who might be suitable to join your team . . .? Well, I think I've finally found someone who fits the bill . . . A Dr April Crump . . . Yes, I'll keep a *very* close eye on her . . .'

2

Avril's Secret Hideaway

Lab One was not, as you might expect, the largest and most important of the laboratories. It was a tiny, shabby room at the top of twelve winding flights of stairs, more like a broom cupboard than a scientific laboratory. There was not enough room to swing a cat in Lab One, though Aunt Primula would probably have given it her best shot, but it was a perfect hideaway for Avril when Leviticus got too much to bear.

Licking her fingers clean of baked beans, Avril reached the top of the stairs. She slotted the key – 'borrowed' from the caretaker – into the lock of Lab One's cobwebbed door, pushed the door open and moved into the dim little room. She made certain to lock the door behind her.

There was no light bulb, and the afternoon light was already fading outside the cracked single window, so Avril had to squint through the gathering gloom. There was the armchair she had dragged up here. There was the old padlocked steel chest that Avril used as a coffee table, already messy with crumbs and packets from her frequent snack attacks. She had never bothered to try to find out what was in the chest: this was Leviticus, after all. It was almost certainly filled with old paperwork, like the stuff that lay crumpled in the lab's corners. Lab One was not exactly a palace, but she didn't care. To Avril, it was luxury itself. A pleasurable little thrill ran through her as she eased herself into the chair and put her feet up on the chest.

Avril reached for her snack box, which she had carefully wrapped in an old labcoat and hidden behind the armchair. She unwrapped it, slid open the wooden lid and selected a large chocolate cupcake, moist and sticky with fudgy icing. There were a few sprinkles of a bluish powder decorating the icing, which Avril took to be tiny hundreds and thousands until she bit into the cake and nearly choked. The blue sprinkles were not hundreds and thousands at all. Heaven only knew *exactly* what they were, but Avril supposed that was one of the hazards of making a snack box out of Uncle Edgar's chemistry set. She hadn't used the old set for years now, but she had not had the heart to throw away the memories of her childhood experiments. One half of the box was still filled with tubes and vials of untouched weird and wonderful chemicals, while the other was stuffed with the cakes and sweets that made Avril feel a little happier on days like these.

Avril brushed off the blue powder and gave the cupcake a second go. She was just pondering a huge jam tart when she remembered the resignation letter. She reached out to pick up an old sheet of paper from the nearest corner, turned it over to the unused side and fished a pen out of her pocket.

Dear Dr Wetherby . . .

Avril was so pleased with the opening of her resignation letter that she allowed herself a celebratory bite of jam tart.

After much thought and careful consideration . . .

Too pompous. Dr Wetherby might think she was imitating him. She scribbled it out and tried again.

I very much regret that I must inform you . . .

Too apologetic. She scribbled some more.

I find myself unable to continue under such conditions . . .

It has come to my notice that my position is no longer tenable . . .

It saddens me from the bottom of my heart that our working relationship . . .

Avril was almost waist-deep in paper when she finally came up with the finished letter nearly half an hour later.

Dear Dr Wetherby
Had enough. You can stuff it.
Avril

She was just checking it for mistakes, and agonising over whether to put a kiss after her signature at the bottom, when she heard footsteps outside. Her first instinct was to stuff the letter into her labcoat pocket, then grab Uncle Edgar's snack box and clutch it protectively to her, as she waited for the footsteps to turn round and go away.

But the footsteps were not about to go away. They belonged to Dr Wetherby, who now stood outside Lab One with an ear pressed to the door. He had followed the trail of pale orange footprints, decorated with the occasional squashed baked bean, which led all the way from the ground floor. Dr Wetherby hated mess. The

Crump woman disgusted him. But she was going to be useful to him now. She had humiliated him in front of Dr Sedukta, and he was going to make her pay.

Dr Wetherby was ambitious. There was a vacant place on Leviticus's Board of Governors, and this obsessed his every waking moment. He wanted that job more than anything. And if he wanted to rise to the lofty heights of Governor he had to find a way to get noticed by the Powers-That-Be. This was where Dr Crump would come in. She was already unpopular enough with the Leviticus chiefs after those explosions; it would not take much to convince them that he had caught her conducting an Unauthorised Experiment as well. He rubbed his hands at the thought of the Governors' gratitude, and pounded on the door with his briefcase.

'Dr Crump? Open this door immediately!'

Inside Lab One, Avril clutched her snack box even tighter. How on earth had he found her?

'Really, Dr Crump, there's no point in hiding. I know you're in there.'

'Just a minute, Dr Wetherby . . .'

Avril's heart was pounding. For all the gung-ho spirit of her resignation letter, she was easily intimidated by her boss. She did not want to have to face him right now.

'Dr Crump, unless you let me in this minute, I will be going straight to the Board of Governors. They don't look kindly on Unauthorised Experiments.'

Avril knew better than to argue with him.

'All right,' she sighed, feeling defeated and turning the key in the lock.

Dr Wetherby pushed Avril out of the way and scanned the old laboratory for evidence of illegal-looking experiments. But there was nothing of interest in here. Just a small armchair and some sort of low coffee table.

'I'm not doing anything wrong, Dr Wetherby,' Avril began. 'I just came up here to get a bit of peace and quiet . . .'

But Dr Wetherby was not listening. He had just noticed that the coffee table was not a table at all – it was in fact some sort of steel chest, bolted with an enormous padlock. *Extremely* suspicious. Could it be a *real* Unauthorised Experiment? This was much better than the baked beans! He could hardly believe his luck!

'What's in this box?' Dr Wetherby straightened up and stared at Avril.

'I've no idea.' Avril was just relieved that it was not a sample resignation letter he had spotted. 'It's locked, and I certainly don't have a key.'

'Ha! A likely story!' Dr Wetherby was already sweeping snack debris off the top of the chest. He pulled at the padlock, and was amazed when it came off in his hand. The metal of the lock was old and rusty, and the chest itself was tarnished and thick with dust. It looked as if it might have been there for many years.

'Open it,' Avril said. She was rather intrigued now, and wishing she had examined it earlier. 'See what's inside.'

'Very clever, Avril.' Dr Wetherby looked at her beadily. 'Pretending you don't know what's in here. Well, it won't wash with me – *or* with the Governors.'

He turned back to the steel box and ran a hand along its dusty lid. There were some words stencilled on the steel. He cleared more dust away, wrinkling his nose in distaste and wiping his hand clean on his labcoat.

Repl Chmb Mk 1.

'*I* don't know what that means,' Avril said, before Dr Wetherby could even ask. She had crouched down beside him to look more closely at the box. 'You'd better open it.'

'*You* open it.' Dr Wetherby did not like to take

unnecessary risks now that there was no Dr Sedukta to impress. His looks were too important to have them ruined by some sort of explosion.

Avril's looks were not of the least importance to her. Besides, she was eager to find out what a Repl Chmb might be.

There was a satisfying clunk as she lifted the lid a couple of centimetres. Dr Wetherby cringed behind her, waiting for the bang. When none came, he peered round and followed Avril's gaze into the box.

It was empty.

Empty except for a handful of chemical beakers in one corner. There were also a few broken-looking switches and a couple of disconnected wires, but nothing more. Avril picked up one of the beakers and studied it more closely. It was filled with a layer of clear gel, but nothing else was visible to the naked eye.

'You don't suppose . . .' Avril stopped. She lowered the lid a little and stared down at the lettering, and then back at the beaker in her hand as a connection between the two began to dawn on her.

'All I am interested in hearing from you, Avril, is a confession.'

'Repl Chmb . . .' Avril murmured to herself. 'I wonder . . .'

Dr Wetherby was rapidly losing what was left of his patience. 'Just tell me precisely what you are doing with this chest!'

'But it isn't mine! I was just thinking . . . wasn't Professor Blut's human-cloning equipment called a Replication Chamber?'

'Professor Blut?' Dr Wetherby blinked. 'What on earth does this have to do with him?'

'Look,' Avril said eagerly, thrusting a beaker under Dr Wetherby's large nose. 'First of all, do you see that gel? There could be human cells suspended in there. And if Repl Chmb stands for anything, it might easily be Replication Chamber. It looks about fifteen years old too,' she mused, 'what with all this dust . . .'

Dr Wetherby's mouth fell open. 'It's even worse than I thought! You're using Professor Blut's old equipment in an attempt to make an illegal human clone!'

'I said nothing of the sort! And anyway, I'm sure the machine doesn't even work after all these years.' Avril gave the chest a little kick.

Deep down inside the box, a chilly blue light suddenly glowed. It flickered off again, then back on.

Avril and Dr Wetherby stared. 'How did that . . .?'

A low hum started up. The Chamber was vibrating gently.

'I've had enough of this!' Dr Wetherby seized Avril by the elbow. 'You're coming with me! I'd like to see you deny *this* to the Board of Governors. Human cloning! You're breaking Rule 149, Rule 837, Directive seventeen of the 1991 Statutes . . . you're in *really* big trouble now, missy!'

'Let go!' Avril struggled, still holding her snack box tightly. 'This has nothing to do with me!'

But Dr Wetherby was not listening. He could already hear the Chief Governor's words: '. . . *A warm welcome to our latest member, Dr Raymond Wetherby* . . .' He was feeling intoxicated at the thought. 'Come on, you hairless lump!' He pulled even harder at her arm.

Avril pulled back.

Dr Wetherby pulled again.

And as the pair of them struggled, Avril's snack box – Uncle Edgar's chemistry set – slipped out of her grasp and was flung into the air. It performed a beautiful little backflip, losing its polished wooden lid and showering its contents everywhere. Orange powder sprayed like a firework. Chocolate cupcakes and cheese muffins rained from the sky. Strange yellow liquid splashed from uncorked tubes. Peculiar purple pellets twirled through the air. And the entire

box, confectionery and all, landed smack in the open Replication Chamber.

There was a colossal, flame-throwing, window-shattering explosion.

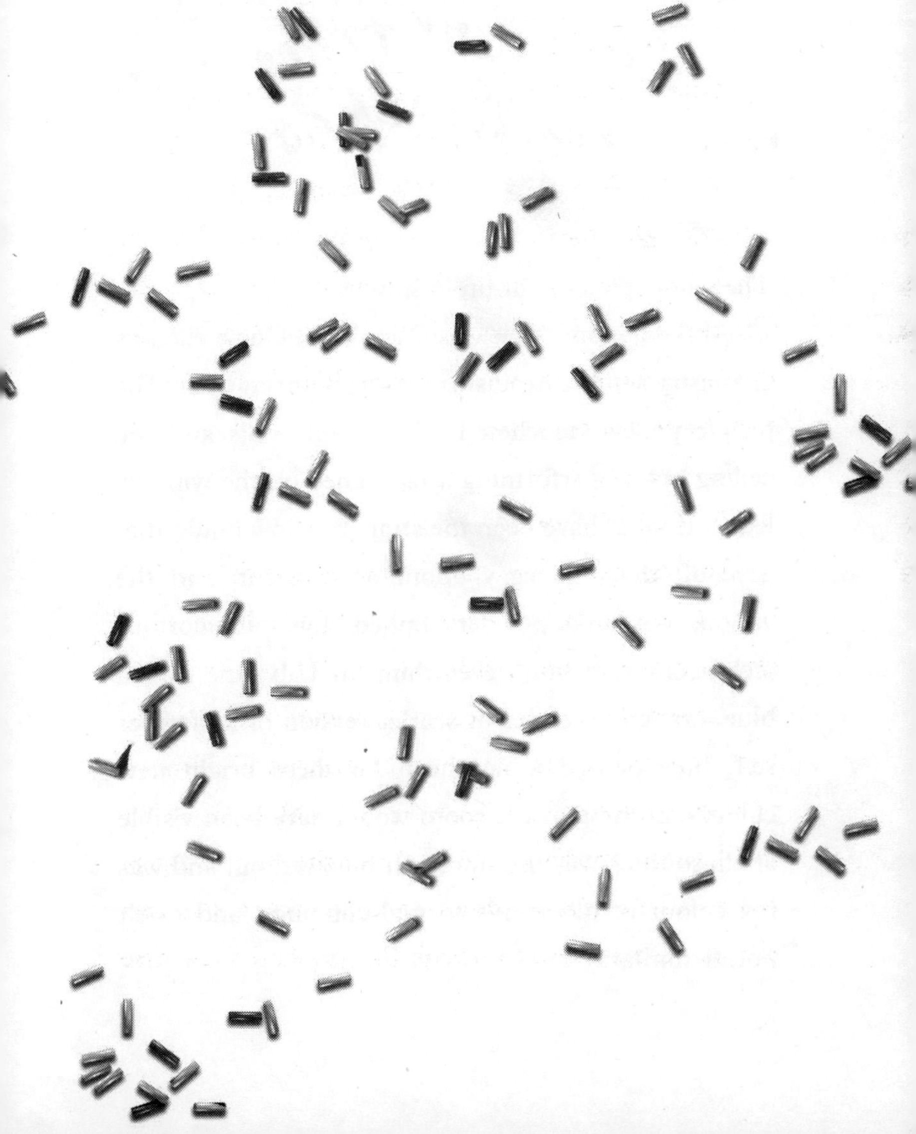

3

Crawling from the Wreckage

The whole place went up in smoke.

And what smoke it was. Thanks to Uncle Edgar's chemistry set, the explosion was truly spectacular. The purple pellets ricocheted off all four walls and the ceiling before performing a tap dance on the window ledge. It must have been the strange yellow liquid that gave off that vile eggy odour as it burnt, and the various coloured powders rained down in glorious technicolour, turning everything in Lab One into a blue, orange, lavender or scarlet version of its former self. Indeed, had it not been for these bright new colours, nothing in the room would have been visible at all, so thick was the smoke. It billowed out and was the colour of old men's toenail clippings, and smelt not dissimilar.

This was a disaster.

Not only was Avril knocked out as her head hit the concrete floor of Lab One. Not only was she now likely to be in real trouble with the Board of Governors. But Uncle Edgar's chemistry set, Avril's most treasured possession, was a burning wreck.

Avril did not remain unconscious for long. After coming to, she lay still for a good ten minutes, trying to sort herself out. She straightened her legs and disentangled them from each other. She rolled over on to her back and checked that all her teeth were intact – the ones that had been intact before the explosion, anyway – and then she slowly began to sit up.

'I'm *blind*!'

Avril was not a woman to panic unnecessarily, so she double-checked that her eyes were open before giving way to hysteria.

'I'M BLIND!' she wailed again. 'I CAN'T SEE!'

She moved on to her hands and knees and began to shuffle about, knocking her bald head on the burning remains of the chair. 'Somebody help me!' she choked. Then she realised that it was the smoke that was making her splutter. That was also why she couldn't see.

This stopped her from panicking. Avril had been involved in too many exploding experiments to worry about a bit of smoke. She slunk down very low to breathe the cleanest air, and tried to remember where the door was. Avril was nothing if not courageous. She began to crawl.

She had not made it more than a metre before her hand touched something soft. Gingerly, she moved it upwards. She was touching something fleshy. It was not altogether pleasant.

'Dr Wetherby!'

She jumped to her feet, ignoring the drowning sensation in her smoke-filled lungs, seized the hand that she had been touching and began to pull.

'Don't worry,' she puffed, pulling with all her not inconsiderable weight. 'I'll save you!' Bellowing like a wrestler, she started to drag the body towards the doorway. 'Just hang on in there!'

Avril was starting to enjoy herself. She felt rather like an action hero.

'Stay with me, bud,' she panted. 'We're gonna get you outta here.'

Unfortunately, one of the unconscious body's large feet hooked itself around the doorframe, and Avril wasted several minutes of tugging before she realised the problem and detached it. With one mighty heave, they were out.

'We've made it!' Avril fell upon her companion in exhaustion. For a moment she was too worn out to speak or move. There she lay in the corridor, splayed in weary triumph, her chest heaving and her eyes watering.

'Get thee off me!'

The quavering cry pierced the smoky air.

'I canst not breathe! Get thee off . . .' It tailed into a weak gurgle.

'Oh, don't be such a wimp, Dr Wetherby,' Avril said. 'It's the smoke in your lungs. That's the reason you can't breathe. It'll clear in a minute. Have a good cough.'

'Nay, nay . . . 'tis thee! What manner of beast *art* thou – some sort of elephant?'

This did not sound like Dr Wetherby. His insults were usually delivered in nasty sneering tones. Not seventeenth-century English.

'Dr Wetherby . . .?'

'I beg thy pardon?'

It was not Dr Wetherby.

Avril turned to look into the face of the person she had rescued. She began to tremble.

The sight before her eyes was extraordinary. The collapsed figure was that of an immensely long and equally scrawny man. His bony frame was clad in some sort of antique black-and-red uniform, with smart epaulettes and a great deal of dazzling medal-work. His face was gaunt, his hair unkempt, his eyes wide. Mesmerised, Avril sat up.

'Hallelujah!' the man gasped, sitting up too. 'Air!'

Avril stared at him. She hiccuped.

'Oh dear! Art thou unwell? Hast thou some malady?' He patted Avril on the back. 'Take thee a deep breath, my lady.'

'*My lady?*' Avril gaped. 'I'm just Avril.'

'Enchanted to make thy acquaintance, Lady Avril!' Now that he wasn't having the life crushed out of him, the man was extremely polite. He extended a hand. Avril shook it. It felt very warm.

'Who *are* you?'

'I know not, but my birth is all thanks to thee, Lady Avril.'

'Well, I suppose . . .' Avril attempted to collect her thoughts. 'I suppose it is thanks to me in a way. Me and Uncle Edgar's chemistry set. Assuming that you've just come out of the Replication Chamber.'

Now it was the man's turn to stare. 'Why, Lady Avril, I believe this explosion has sent thee a bit funny in the head.' He scrambled to his feet. Vertical, he looked even taller. He was at least seven feet high. 'Prithee . . .?' He reached out to help Avril stand up. 'I have a suggestion, Lady Avril. Let us repair to a simple tavern or hostelry. A hearty plate of stew is just what thou needest.'

Avril was not listening. She reached up as far as she could and touched his face. 'A *human clone . . .*'

The clone blinked. He opened his mouth to speak, displaying unhealthy-looking grey teeth. Before a word emerged, however, there was a noise from inside Lab One.

'HELP!'

Avril and the clone looked at each other. Neither moved.

'*HELP!*'

It was louder this time. There was no mistaking it. And although it was a male voice, it was definitely *not* Dr Wetherby's.

'Oh, fine, *don't* help then. I'll just lie here in an exploding room facing certain violent death, shall I?'

'Gadzooks!' The clone's arm shot into the air, a bony finger pointing to the source of the voice. '*There's somebody else in there.*'

'There's no need to worry about me!' came the voice. 'I can die horribly any time.'

The incredibly tall man let out a shriek. 'He will die, Lady Avril! We must save him! Tell me what to do!'

Deep in the recesses of Avril's stupefied mind, something clicked. She felt a powerful sensation course through her. It started at her toes and sprinted upwards, making her bald head tingle. If she'd had hair, it would have stood on end. There was at least one more clone in there.

'Lady Avril,' her companion whimpered. 'He will perish.'

Avril gathered herself together.

'Stay low,' she instructed the man.

He nodded down at her from a great height.

'On second thoughts,' Avril corrected herself, 'just take a very deep breath.'

The clone took an enormous gulp of air. He burped gently. Then he tried again. Cheeks puffed outwards, eyes already bulging, he held out his hand. Avril laced her stubby fingers through his spindly ones and squeezed.

'Let's go.'

4

And Eddy Makes Three

The smoke in Lab One was no longer pea-soup thick. The explosions had diminished to feeble popping. It was into this eerily calm atmosphere that Avril and the clone stepped, hand in hand.

There was something in the middle of the room. It could have been some*one*, but it was still quite hard to make anything out. Perhaps it was Dr Wetherby. Avril peered through the wisps of smoke.

'Wow,' she said. 'This smoke is toxic stuff. It's making me think I can see a *dog* down there on the floor.'

'Woof woof,' came a sarcastic voice.

'By thunder!' The tall, spindly clone's face glowed white. 'A talking dog!'

Sprawled comfortably on the floor, propping itself

up on Uncle Edgar's overturned chemistry set with a paw supporting its head, lay a medium-sized, floppy-eared, mud-brown dog. There were no two ways about it. It was canine. And it spoke.

'Anyway, thanks for showing up.' It yawned. It crossed its two hind legs and glanced languidly at its left paw. It appeared to be inspecting its claws. 'Nasty situation here. This smoke is very unpleasant.'

Avril finally found her voice. She'd been searching for the usual one, her familiar blend of boom and squeak, rather than the strangled tones that now emerged.

'Do you need rescuing?' she asked.

The dog's right ear pricked up.

'If you would,' it said. It gave a small cough. 'Bad for the lungs, you know.'

'Hast thou broken a leg?' gasped the tall clone. 'Canst thou not walk? Allow me to lift thee, Mr . . . er . . . Dog . . . and I shall bear thee from this place to safety!'

The dog stretched out luxuriantly. 'All right. Get bearing.'

'You don't *look* injured,' Avril said.

'Injured?' echoed the dog. 'Not in the least. Though thanks only to my dazzling display of quick thinking and nimbleness. Dodging burning missiles isn't child's play, you know.'

'So if you're not injured,' Avril continued, 'why couldn't you just escape yourself? Why all the yelling for help?' She felt quite cross, mostly on behalf of the poor, panic-stricken tall clone.

The dog looked slightly abashed – but only for a moment. 'Well,' it said airily, 'I do have a *small* injury. Could be a shattered spine or a wrenched pelvis. Nothing serious. I didn't even think to mention it.' It squeezed out a brave tear.

'My dear fellow!' The clone gathered the dog up in his arms like a baby. 'Fret not!'

The dog swung its tail. 'I'll try not to. Oh,' it added, nodding at Avril, 'you ought to get on with rescuing that girl in the corner. *She* hasn't looked too healthy for a while.'

Avril spun round.

A little girl! There she lay, curled up in the corner of Lab One as though she were having a quiet afternoon nap.

Avril sank to her knees and grabbed the girl's wrist. A pulse! A good, steady pulse. She was not only alive, she was well.

'Uurrgggh.'

And she could talk! 'Uurrgggh' wasn't exactly an articulate turn of phrase, but at least she hadn't barked. Avril shook her vigorously, desperate to wake her up. The girl opened her eyes.

'Strange dream,' she said. She stared at Avril and blinked. 'Am I awake now?'

Avril gazed back at her – the shiny, straight, light-brown hair, the fresh eyes, the friendly button nose. She smiled.

'You're awake,' she said. She picked up the singed old labcoat that her snack box had been wrapped in and carefully placed it around the little girl's shoulders before holding out a hand to help her stand. 'Now, let's go somewhere we can talk.'

'Prithee, madam,' piped up the tall, bony clone, 'should we assist this poor gentleman?'

He was pointing at the floor, where a dozing Dr Wetherby lay.

'Oh, no,' Avril said, leading the clones from Lab One. 'He'll be quite all right for a little longer. We'll come back for him later.'

Out in the corridor, Dr Sedukta smoothed her long hair, pulled the mobile phone from her pocket and dialled a number.

‘It’s me again,’ she whispered. ‘You won’t *believe* what I’ve just seen . . .’

Next door to Lab One was a large broom cupboard. There was plenty of room for Avril and the clones to sit on upturned buckets and talk.

‘Right.’ Avril took a deep breath and tried to look capable. She felt completely responsible for these poor clones. ‘First things first. This . . . er . . . this is a very unusual situation,’ she began.

Perched imperiously on his bucket (his spine and pelvis looking in mint condition), the dog snorted.

‘Let’s begin,’ Avril continued, ‘with a few introductions. Get to know each other a bit. I’m Avril Crump. I’m a scientist . . . I like insects . . . I’m trying to create a miracle sponge that mops up oil spills . . . My favourite colour is green . . . er . . . I’ve got a little green vintage convertible sports car – that means I can drive around with the roof down . . .’ Avril thought hard. ‘I like doughnuts . . . er . . .’ She gave up. ‘I’m sorry,’ she said. ‘It doesn’t sound very exciting. I’m still in shock, I think. I can’t believe I’m sitting here talking to three clones.’

There was a pause.

The girl spoke. ‘Sorry, Avril, but what’s a *clone*?

I'm not sure we understand.'

'Do we even want to?' said the dog.

Avril moved forward on her bucket, eager to explain. 'Cloning is a way of duplicating a living organism so it has exactly the same characteristics as the original. Same DNA. That means,' she said, catching the girl's confused expression, 'same face, same body, same everything. It's already been done with animals – sheep, rats . . . spiders,' she added rather wistfully. 'But cloning a person . . . well, that's quite a different matter. It's never been done before. But there was a scientist here years ago called Professor Blut who wanted to be the first to clone a human. A *perfect* human. It seems, however, to have gone slightly wrong.'

The tall, thin clone sniffed sadly. 'Meanest thou that we are *im*perfect?'

Avril put a reassuring hand on his arm. 'That's not it,' she said. 'I just mean that he was trying to put together a sort of super-human. I'm sure the three of you have all sorts of wonderful talents! People say that Professor Blut raided graves for toenails and hairs to get the DNA he needed. Like William Shakespeare's, for example.' The clones were looking blank. 'He was a brilliant playwright, so you'll probably all be ever so good at . . . er . . . reading and writing . . .' Avril tried to think of all the staffroom whispers she had overheard about Professor Blut's experiment. 'Oh, and you might have the cells of a famous general named Napoleon . . . although now I think about it –' she eyed the dog nervously – 'perhaps it's a hair from his cherished pet instead.' Avril's voice tailed off.

The girl was staring straight at her. 'Do you mean to say,' she said, 'that we are a hotch-potch?'

'Not a hotch-potch exactly, more a . . .'

'A rag-bag of odds and ends? A cocktail of bits and pieces?'

Avril was feeling very small. 'That's not what I meant to . . .'

'Well, I think that's *fantastic.*' The girl beamed at her two fellow clones. The thin man beamed back and the dog grimaced. 'Isn't that lovely?' the girl continued. 'To be a mixture of all those wonderful people! We must know all sorts of things! A playwright, you say? Is that why he,' she pointed at the man, 'talks like that?'

'I suppose so,' Avril said. 'Though how he's ended up wearing that uniform is completely beyond me.'

'Oh, get a life.' The dog yawned. 'Who *cares* about his choice of outfit?'

'And this dog,' the girl said. 'Am I right in thinking that dogs can't usually talk?'

'Yeah, right,' said the dog scornfully. 'A dog that can't talk? What parallel universe are *you* living in?'

'This is so cool!' the girl said. Her eyes were shining. Avril noticed that one eye was sea-green while the other gleamed warm amber. What with that and her rosy cheeks, her face bore a charming resemblance to a set of traffic lights. 'I mean, we're totally unique,' she continued. 'And *nobody*'s done this before – cloned someone?'

'Not until now. It isn't even allowed.'

The girl's face fell. 'Not *allowed*? Are we in some sort of trouble?'

'Of course not.' Avril patted her hand. 'It's not your fault that Blut was trying to create human clones.'

'Humans, humans, humans.' The dog's shoulders drooped mournfully. 'I'm starting to feel like a second-class citizen here.' He gave a loud sniff.

'Oh, Mr Dog, thou art not second class!' The tall clone stroked the dog's tail.

'Don't be nice to me . . .' The dog's voice wobbled. 'It's the tenderness I can't bear.' He burst into noisy sobs.

Avril and the girl exchanged a glance.

'I wouldn't mind so much –' the dog turned to the tall clone, sensing an ally – 'if I felt that I was being taken seriously. I mean, I haven't even been given a name, for pity's sake!' An enormous tear fell on to the floor. The dog looked rather pleased with himself before hurriedly rearranging his features.

'But Mr Dog –'

'Don't you see,' the dog interrupted, 'that calling me *Mr Dog* simply increases my feeling of isolation?' He cast a baleful glance at his companions, sank miserably on to his hind legs, put his paws over his eyes and stayed very still.

'He's right,' Avril said, not unmoved by the dog's pitiful posture. 'You *should* have names. But I'm afraid I have no ideas at all. You should pick names for yourselves.'

'Oh, no,' the girl said. 'It'd feel so much nicer if you chose for us.' She looked at the tall clone for support.

He nodded vigorously.

Avril felt a warm glow in her middle, as though someone had just lit a birthday cake inside her. The glow spread upwards. She was blushing.

'Gosh . . . er . . . well . . . names . . . absolutely . . .'

'See?' The dog raised his head for a moment,

possibly to show off the second huge teardrop he had manufactured. 'She can't think of names for us *at all*.'

'Bonaparte!' The word sprang from Avril's lips.

She pointed at the tall clone. He looked as surprised as she did.

'Bonaparte?' he asked.

'Yes, Bonaparte.' Avril said. 'It was Napoleon's other name.'

'It's perfect,' said the girl.

'Plus,' added the dog, his voice muffled by the paws over his head, 'it can be shortened to Bony.'

The tall clone's lips moved as he silently tried out his new name. Then a smile appeared. It was the broadest thing about him.

'Bonaparte,' he said. He got to his feet and gave a deep bow, bumping his head on the ground. 'At thy service.'

'What about me?' The girl sounded rather shy.

Avril thought very hard. She ran through her colleagues at Leviticus before realising that she did not know what any of them were really called. She couldn't name this little girl *Doctor*. Maybe there was something suitable she could remember from her childhood. The girls at school had often had pretty-sounding names, if she could recall . . . 'Let's see . . . Mary? Susan? Jessica?' The trouble was that, though the names were pretty, the memories of their owners were not. *Avril Crump's a bald, fat lump* rang in her ears. She bit her lip. 'Let's think of something else . . . Primula, perhaps? Heavens, no! Not *that* individual.' Avril groped the air a little, as though trying to pluck the right name from it. Her eyes glazed with concentration. Suddenly her fist snapped shut somewhere above her bald head. 'Edna!'

'Edna?' The girl looked perturbed. 'Do you not think . . . maybe, Mary . . .?'

'No, no!' Avril radiated pleasure. 'Edna is perfect! How could I have forgotten it? When I was a little girl, *all* my toys were called Edna.'

'All your dolls and stuff?' the girl said, extremely doubtfully.

'Dolls . . .' Avril waved a hand vaguely, recalling the terrible fate of the one and only doll she'd ever been given. 'Teddy bears, cuddly dragons, wind-up cars, train sets . . .' She sighed. 'Many a happy hour I spent with Edna the Engine.'

'It's a nice name.' The girl was diplomatic. 'But perhaps I could shorten it. *Eddy* isn't too bad.'

'Edna, Eddy, whatever . . . Lovely, lovely!' Avril clapped her hands. 'Now . . .' She turned to the dog. 'This is a tricky one.'

'No, it isn't.' The dog's voice was muffled. 'Augustus.'

Bonaparte handed him his handkerchief.

The dog raised his head and fixed him with a hard stare.

'It wasn't a *sneeze*. It's my *name*. Augustus,' he repeated. 'Like the Roman emperor. In fact, I think I may have a dash or two of Roman emperor in me.' He flicked his tail. 'What do you say? The pride of my bearing, the nobility of my profile, the terror –' he gave Avril a stare – 'of my gaze?'

'Well,' Avril said, 'I don't think there was any Roman emperor in the cloning mix. But perhaps . . .'

The dog held up a paw to silence Avril. 'Roman emperors,' he said, 'are *born*, not *made*.'

'Your Highness!' Overwhelmed, Bonaparte gave another sweeping bow, this time avoiding the floor. 'I am indeed honoured to be in thy imperial presence! We are unfit to breathe your air, my liege, and yet in thy magnanimity and greatness of spirit, thou communest with us, thy poor servants!'

'Yes, well . . .' The dog looked faintly uncomfortable

at this display of adulation. 'My name is Augustus. So there you are.'

'There we are indeed,' said Avril, sensing that Bonaparte might launch into another embarrassing speech. 'So . . .' She looked around at the three clones and scratched her head. 'What do we do now?'

It came out sounding more worried than she had intended. But really, she was at a complete loss. All she knew was that the clones were her responsibility. She couldn't just abandon them, leave them to fend for themselves. Besides, she was starting to feel extremely fond of them. She had never been needed like this before, and the warm glow in her middle felt wonderful. It was better than any doughnut she had ever eaten.

'Right.' This time her voice was confident. 'Here's the plan. I'm going to have to hide you somewhere. We'll wait until tonight and then I can smuggle you out of here, under cover of darkness, and drive you to my house in Wretchford-on-the-Reeke. You'll be safe there with me.'

'Your house?' Augustus looked dubious.

'Thank you so much, Avril,' Eddy said. 'I'm sure we'll be safe with you to look after us.'

Avril smiled. This would be so much fun. She

would take care of these clones as well as she knew how, from the roof over their head to the food in their mouths. Which, come to think of it . . .

'First things first,' she said, for the second time that day. Except that now she knew exactly what ought to come first. 'Tea time.'

5

Escape from Leviticus

Dr Wetherby came round slowly, and was in a foul temper before he was even fully awake. He remembered exactly how he had been knocked out, and he knew exactly who to blame for it.

He ran his hands over his face, checking his nose, his teeth, his hairline. It all felt all right, but he would find a mirror as soon as possible. There was an infuriating ringing in his ears that only got worse as he hauled himself to his feet, but at least his looks seemed intact. He would go and find Avril Crump and give her a piece of his mind, before dragging her off to face the Governors. It would be even more impressive if he took some actual evidence of this Unauthorised Experiment with him. Pity most of it was now on fire. He hunted about for anything that was not in flames. That charred lump of wood would do, he thought, picking it up with his handkerchief. It was the remains of that box Dr Crump had dropped on the Replication Chamber. Perfect. This would incriminate her nicely. Dr Wetherby located his briefcase, which, though smouldering, had been thrown clear of the worst of the explosion, and popped the evidence inside.

He tried out a couple of limps as he left Lab One, wondering which would win him the most sympathy. Maybe getting caught up in this explosion was not such a bad thing. He could wear a heroic-looking bandage to his inauguration ceremony, maybe even carry a crutch. *That* would have Dr Sedukta swooning, all right. He was feeling so pleased with himself that he almost missed the voices coming from the broom cupboard.

Treading softly in his rubber-soled shoes, Dr Wetherby backed up the stairs and went to the cupboard. He crouched a little and pressed his ear against the door.

'No, no!' It was Avril's booming voice. 'Edna is perfect! How could I have forgotten it? When I was a little girl, *all* my toys were called Edna.'

What sort of certifiable lunatic, Dr Wetherby

thought, named *all* their toys Edna? And who on earth was she talking to?

'. . . I think I may have a dash or two of Roman emperor in me . . .'

Who was *that*? Dr Wetherby hoped nobody had followed him up here. They might have seen him struggling with Avril, and would know that he had helped to cause the explosion.

'. . . I don't think there was any Roman emperor in the cloning mix . . .'

Cloning mix?

Dr Wetherby pressed his ear even more tightly against the door. He was concentrating so intently that he didn't notice the silent figure of Dr Sedukta lurking in the shadows at the end of the hallway, watching him.

'Dr Wetherby!'

Dr Wetherby straightened up and looked down at Avril, who had just opened the door.

'Yes,' he said. 'It is I.'

Avril shuffled backwards. 'I'm so sorry, Dr Wetherby.' She swallowed. 'I was going to come back in to find you, but . . .'

'Perhaps you were saving *somebody else*?'

Avril's wide eyes were all the answer he needed.

'Let me see what you're hiding,' he demanded, shoving at Avril.

'Absolutely not!' Avril said. 'Hand them over to you so you can go straight to the Governors with them?'

'*Them?* Who are you hiding in there? Let me in!'

'No!' Avril pulled the door shut behind her.

'How dare you defy Raymond Wetherby!' Dr Wetherby shouted. 'You will regret this!' He seized Avril by the sleeve and tried to hustle her towards the stairs. 'If you won't let me in, perhaps you might be more willing to offer an explanation to the police!'

Avril stood her ground. 'No!'

'Dr Crump, you are in very big trouble. Whether you let me in or not, your little secret will get out. But perhaps if you cooperate, we might be able to keep this within Leviticus. If we handle this in the proper manner, the police need not be involved . . .'

Avril felt sick with anxiety. If Dr Wetherby got his hands on the clones, she would never see them again. Fearing a scandal, the Governors would destroy them, of that she was certain. 'I can't . . . I won't . . .'

'Oh, for heaven's sake!' Dr Wetherby took advantage of Avril's confusion. He darted around her and managed to push the door halfway open before she had time to stop him.

'Good grief,' came a voice. 'How many more introductions must we endure?'

A talking dog. There was no regulation to deal with this. Dr Wetherby's eyes boggled. He staggered backwards.

Avril seized the opportunity. '*Run!*' she yelled at the clones, giving Dr Wetherby a shove that unbalanced him further. 'Get out of here!'

'No!' Dr Wetherby steadied himself. 'You stay right where you are!' He reached out to grab Bonaparte just as Avril delivered a brisk punch to his large nose. He howled. 'Is it broken?' He brought his hands up to his face. 'Tell me it's not broken!'

'Go!' Avril ordered Eddy. 'I'll take care of him. Just run!'

Dr Wetherby lunged for Avril and began trying to wrestle her to the floor, a job which he regretted almost as soon as he had started. Not only was she even heavier than he had thought earlier, but the dog suddenly rushed at him. Before he could react, the animal had leapt straight at his head, snarling. A paw went right into his injured nose. This time, he *really* howled. He knocked Augustus sideways into the wall.

'Mr Dog!'

But there was no time for Bonaparte to reach Augustus. Dr Wetherby had grabbed hold of the tall clone's leg and was trying to drag him out of the broom cupboard.

Eddy grabbed Bonaparte's other arm and began to pull him back just as Avril, thinking fast, seized a bucket and brought it down on Dr Wetherby's head. He let go of Bonaparte.

'Go!' Avril gasped, her eyes meeting Eddy's and Bonaparte's. 'Go, or they'll destroy you all!'

Eddy's eyes widened in horror. She grabbed Bonaparte by the hand and, pausing only for Bony to gather up the crumpled body of the dog, the clones ran.

Dr Wetherby, reeling from the bucket assault, shoved Avril as hard as he knew how. Her head hit the hard floor. As he rebounded backwards, so did his. They lay still, knocked out for the second time that afternoon.

At the end of the hallway, Dr Sedukta slipped out of the shadows and headed for the stairs. She could hear the clones clattering down about four flights ahead of her, and sped up slightly, taking the stairs two at a time in her clacking high-heeled shoes.

* * *

'Miss Eddy!' Bonaparte gasped, clutching Augustus under one arm and waving the other hysterically. 'I hear footsteps! I do believe that man is following us!'

Eddy could also hear the footsteps. They were getting closer. 'Come on!' She sprang up on to the banister and motioned for Bonaparte to do the same. 'It'll be quicker this way . . .'

The banister was smooth with age and provided no resistance. Off they shot, round and round the remaining flights, Bonaparte's long hair and Augustus's ears flying out behind them. Eddy was worrying about what would happen when they reached the bottom. She was still worrying as they sped off the end of the banister, went straight through an open window, and plunged at high speed into a large dustcart.

Spitting out rancid tomato pips and wiping raw egg from her eyes, Eddy shifted sideways before Bonaparte and Augustus could land on top of her.

'Quiet, Bony!' she hissed, as Bonaparte yelped. 'If we stay in here he'll go straight past us.'

Bonaparte nodded obediently.

'This is so undignified!' came a loud voice from inside his coat. Augustus's head popped up. It was topped with a rotting banana skin.

Eddy clamped a hand over the dog's mouth and waited for the clicking footsteps to draw near. Nothing happened for a moment. Then the dustcart suddenly lurched. It felt as though they were being wheeled away.

Dr Sedukta reached the bottom of the stairs. Despite the gathering gloom, she could see well through her large sunglasses. There was no one in sight, except for some filthy maintenance man wheeling a dustcart outside the window. The clones must have slipped into one of the empty labs. Well, after her latest mobile phone conversation, her instructions were clear. She was disappointed that it was not to be an assassination mission, her particular speciality, but perhaps the boss would allow her to have a little more fun after she had captured the clones and delivered them to him.

She took out her phone and re-dialled.

'Me again,' she whispered. 'I'm on the case. But I think you should send someone round here to do a tidy-up. You don't want anyone finding out what happened in Lab One. Oh,' she added, before switching off, 'and send someone to pick up Crump and Wetherby. You should get them to the Manor before they wake up and start blabbing about all this. Then you can decide what to do with them.'

She slipped the phone back into her pocket and set off down the corridor. Finding the clones would not take her very long.

6

The Merry Traveller's Rest

The night air was getting chillier by the minute. The road that had led the clones away from Leviticus Laboratories did not seem to lead *to* anywhere. It was simply going downhill. They were trudging down a deserted country lane with open fields on either side. With no hedge to protect them, the wind whipped up speed and stung their hands and faces. It was freezing cold, and they were going nowhere. Worst of all, a small icicle had begun to take shape on the end of Bonaparte's nose.

'We've been walking for *hours*,' Augustus whined.

'Correction.' Eddy stuffed her blue-tipped fingers into her pockets. An inhospitable fog lay like a thin and stained blanket over the valley into which they were descending. '*We've* been walking for hours.

You've been carried since you decided walking disagreed with you.'

Bonaparte stopped the dirge-like tune he had been humming for the last hour and spoke before Augustus could. 'Oh, no, Miss Eddy, 'twas a selfless act on the part of Mr Dog. He saw how I did shiver and sought to warm me.' To prove his point, Bonaparte pulled open the lapel of his red coat, where Augustus was snuggled. The banana skin still adorned his head. He gave Eddy a reproachful look.

'You see,' he said. 'Bony understands.'

'Here, Miss Eddy.' Bonaparte spoke warmly, eager to keep his friends happy. 'Have thee a nibble of this.' He handed her the withered banana skin from Augustus's head.

'Hey! How long has that been on my head?'

'For about as long as you've selflessly been keeping Bony warm,' said Eddy. 'Now, let's keep our eyes peeled. We have to find somewhere to sleep.'

She was starting to feel very alone. Bonaparte and Augustus seemed oblivious to the danger they were in, but she was frightened and unable to show it. Now that they were separated from Avril, Eddy felt that she was responsible for the other two, and that it was up to her to find shelter. They could not walk all night.

‘A light! Miss Eddy, I do see a light!’

Bonaparte’s long and spindly finger was pointing ahead through the thick fog. Sure enough, now that they were getting closer, Eddy could see a light too. More than one light – a cluster!

‘It must be a town! In the valley! Come on!’

‘I knew that banana skin was there all along,’ Augustus muttered as they put on a burst of speed. ‘I was simply humouring you. Plus it happened to look rather fetching on me. I have the natural style, you see, to carry off the fruit peel look in a way that others never could.’

The town was not as far away as it looked through the disorientating fog and, within minutes, the clones were hurrying past a road sign welcoming them to Wretchford-on-the-Reeke, and advising them to drive carefully.

‘This is where Avril said she lives, do you remember?’ Eddy could hardly believe they were actually having a stroke of luck. ‘Oh, this is wonderful! I’m sure we can find somewhere warm to sleep, and then we’ll track down Avril in the morning.’

However, finding a place to stay began to look tricky as they continued along the gloomy, lamp-lit, tree-lined road into Wretchford. Rambling old houses loomed out of the fog, but not a single light burned in their cracked windows, making Eddy lose the courage to knock on a door.

Augustus peeped out of Bonaparte's jacket as they walked along the deserted street. 'Look at this place! What a dump! *I* think we should carry on and find a more suitable town. Who made you the boss, anyway?' he demanded of Eddy.

'I'm not the boss, Gus,' Eddy said. Her voice rose slightly. 'I'm just trying to find us somewhere safe to sleep!'

'The name,' Augustus said, 'is *Augustus*. Not *Gus*. *Never* Gus.'

Bonaparte suddenly stopped. A small side road led off to the right while the main road stretched off ahead of them into the darkness. 'Which way, Miss Eddy?'

Eddy peered down the side road. It was hard to see very far with the fog clouding over the streetlights, but the houses here looked smaller, neater and more lived in. As a patch of fog cleared for a moment, she suddenly saw that one of the lights was not a street-lamp at all. It shone out of the upstairs window of the second little house on the right. Moving closer, Eddy noticed the rusty sign suspended by the front door. It creaked as it swung to and fro.

'*The Merry Traveller's Rest*,' Eddy read. 'Well, that's a nice name.'

'What else does it say?' Augustus demanded. 'I could read it myself if I wanted,' he added hastily, 'having the DNA of Shakespeare and all that. It's just this fog . . .'

'*Bed and Breakfast*,' Eddy continued. '*All welcome*. This is perfect!' She moved closer to the sign to read the smaller lettering underneath a telephone number. '*No salesmen, actors, little boys, budgerigars, amorous young couples, beards, Manchester United fans, poets, ignoramuses or coffee drinkers*.' In red paint someone had added '*or blithering idiots*' in a violent scrawl. 'Well,' Eddy said, 'seeing as we are none of those things . . . I think . . . there shouldn't be a problem.'

'Surely there's somewhere else to try,' Augustus said, rather nervously. 'I'm not at all sure Bony isn't a Manchester United fan. Whatever that is.'

Eddy thought for a moment. The night was getting colder by the second, and the icicle on Bonaparte's nose was growing rapidly. They would have to take a risk. She marched forward and rang the bell.

Bonaparte's voice filled the ensuing silence. 'I wish it said *Bed and Stew*,' he whispered.

Just then, the front door was flung open. A

bright light shone in the clones' faces.

'What?' The light moved sharply from Eddy to Bonaparte and back again. It was so dazzling that its owner's face could not be seen.

'Er . . . Good evening,' said Eddy. 'We are sorry to disturb you, but my – er – uncle and I . . . and our dog . . . are looking for a place to stay for the night.'

'What sort of dog?' snapped the voice.

'A talking one!' Bonaparte said, followed swiftly by an 'Ouch!' as Eddy kicked him in the ankle.

'A Tor Kin Wan . . . It's a rare Oriental breed . . . Guard dog to the emperors of Japan . . .' Eddy bit her lip. Even to her ears it sounded pathetic. But she mustn't reveal anything, especially not to a complete stranger. Avril had said enough about human cloning for her to realise how dangerous that could be. 'Can we come in?'

The light was lowered as the owner of the Bed and Breakfast stepped closer. Now that they were not being dazzled, the clones saw a wild-haired, scowling man wearing yellow pyjamas decorated with bright green frogs. He scrutinised Eddy, then stared at Augustus for a long moment.

'A Tor Kin Wan, you say?'

Eddy swallowed. 'Well, you may not have heard

of them. They're extremely rare . . .'

'The dog can stay.' The strange man snatched Augustus out of Bonaparte's arms. 'A Tor Kin Wan is just the sort of guest this place needs. As for the pair of *you,* the sign is perfectly clear – no Manchester United fans.' He glared at Eddy. 'And absolutely *no* blithering idiots.' With a jab in the direction of Bonaparte, the man turned and went inside. He was still holding Augustus. The door slammed.

'Mr Dog!' Bonaparte shrieked.

'Don't!' Eddy said. 'Augustus might call back if he hears you. Let me handle this.' She rapped at the door again.

'*Go away!*'

'But, sir . . .' Eddy's teeth were beginning to chatter with cold. 'You've got it wrong. We're not blithering idiots *or* Manchester United fans. We don't even know what Manchester United fans are.'

'In that case –' syrupy sweet, the man opened the door an inch and peered out at them – 'you must be ignoramuses. And goodness me –' he waved his arm up at the sign – 'looks like you're *still* not allowed in.'

The door slammed again.

'Right.' Eddy pounded on it. 'Open up this instant! You've stolen our dog, and unless you return him immediately, we're going to go straight to the police and have you charged with dognapping!'

'Huzzah!' Bonaparte added. ''Tis terribly exciting.'

'Just push off!' snapped the man. 'There is no room for the likes of you in this establishment.'

'Good thing too,' came Augustus's muffled voice.

There was silence. Then the door was flung open. The man stared at them.

'Who said that?'

Glaring at Augustus, who was looking sheepish, Eddy considered her options. Pretend the man was hearing things . . . Claim to be a world-famous ventriloquist . . . Stamp on his toes, grab Augustus and run . . .

'The dog can talk.' The words tumbled out before she could stop them. 'He's not my uncle. I'm not his niece. My name's Eddy, and he's Bonaparte. The dog's Augustus. We're clones from Leviticus Laboratories. Something went wrong and we appeared out of thin air. We're fleeing from a maniac who wants to destroy us. We're in danger of our lives,' she continued, 'and we've only *been* alive a few hours.'

Very slowly, millimetre by millimetre, the man's jaw dropped.

'Prithee,' Bonaparte said, 'return Mr Dog and

we shall never trouble thee more.'

Jaw still hanging, the man turned to gaze at Augustus, who was warming himself by the fire. 'A talking dog,' he managed, 'and a Tor Kin Wan at that . . . incredible.'

'*Please*,' Eddy said. She felt close to tears. 'It's very cold. We have to find somewhere else to stay.'

'Leviticus, you say? And you're running away . . .' The man looked thoughtful for a moment. Then he smiled. His face crinkled into comfortable lines. 'You can't start wandering about the town at this hour. Besides, does it say *no clones* anywhere on that sign?'

'Well, no, but . . .'

'So come in out of the cold! We can't stand about gossiping all night. My name's Lionel, by the way. Now, I've got a bit of stew inside that I think you'll enjoy.'

With a whimper of delight, Bonaparte bounded through the open door.

'Thank you.' Eddy blinked at the man. Now that someone was being nice to her, it was hard to hold back tears of relief. 'This is very kind.'

'Not a bit of it. Anyone running from Leviticus Laboratories is welcome in my home. I've got a thing or two I could tell you about that mob,' he added. 'Now, hurry on in. Anybody could be listening . . .'

He ushered Eddy inside, and shut the door against the freezing night.

The first thing Avril noticed as she came round was the low rumbling noise. It was probably Professor Kobayashi from Astrophysics practising his cello in the library again. Well, she couldn't wait around listening. She had to get after those clones.

It was only when she opened her eyes and tried to get up that she realised that she was not at Leviticus. She was lying face down in a car boot, and the low rumbling was an engine.

She told herself to stay calm and think. The trouble was that her head was pounding, still sore from her meeting with a hard concrete floor. In addition to this her body felt unnaturally heavy, as though she had been drugged. She was struggling to stay awake.

'Hey!' she called, pounding weakly on the lid of the boot. 'You can't do this to me, Dr Wetherby! This is kidnapping!'

But, Avril suddenly thought through the haze, didn't Dr Wetherby drive a small, second-hand car? Yet this car boot was enormous, and the engine was purring expensively. And how had he managed to lift her fifteen-stone bulk all by himself?

As Avril sank again into her drugged sleep, somebody began to whistle in the front of the car.

It was not Dr Wetherby.

7

Lionel's Conspiracies

Lionel's living room was tiny, and rather a mess. There was just one armchair in front of the open fire, in which Augustus was already ensconced. He was dozing.

'One moment, please.' Lionel produced a thin metallic device from a drawer and proceeded to wave it behind Bonaparte's ears and the backs of his knees. He did the same for Eddy before nodding with relief and replacing the device. 'Bug detector,' he explained. 'You can never be too careful.'

Eddy did not really know what he was talking about, but she was too tired to care. Somebody else was taking charge now.

'I know what you're thinking.' Lionel was bustling about fetching cushions for Eddy and Bonaparte to sit on, and going in and out of a small and very grimy-looking kitchen with a pot and some plates. 'Doesn't look much like a Bed and Breakfast.'

Eddy had not been thinking this, but she smiled politely. She took the plate of stew he was offering her and passed it along to Bonaparte, who fell on it with a little cry.

'Well, it's not.' He lowered his voice. 'That's just my cover story. I need to look like I'm employed, so I can keep an eye on things around here without raising suspicion.'

'What things?' Eddy asked, accepting a plate of stew for herself.

'That retirement home across the road, for starters.' Lionel's voice dropped to a whisper and he peeped around the curtain. 'That's why I moved here. No one believes me, but there's an international organised-crime unit operating out of there.'

'Really?' Eddy tasted her stew. It was surprisingly good.

'But I mustn't say too much.' Lionel was studying her. 'You seem like a bright girl,' he said. 'Did you see anything suspicious up at Leviticus?'

'Whole place was suspicious, if you ask me.' Augustus opened one eye and held out a paw for stew. 'Unpleasant explosions and horrible smelly dustcarts.'

'Exactly!' Lionel slammed a triumphant fist on the filthy coffee table. Stew splattered. 'The whole place *is* suspicious! And now here you three are. *Human clones.* Well, two humans and a Tor Kin Wan. I've suspected human cloning's been going on for some time, of course. You only have to look at those suspicious so-called "boy bands".' He made quotation marks in the air with his fingers. 'Always five members, always three who can't sing, two who can't dance. Terrible white suits. Don't tell me there's not something funny going on there. I've always said it. But no one on the force would listen. I used to be a policeman. The scourge of crime in Wretchford,' he added sadly. 'Of course, I haven't worked for nearly twenty years now. None of that young lot at the station even knows who I am.'

'Did you retire?' Eddy asked.

'Retire? If only!' He stared round at them. 'Can you keep secrets?'

'Oh, indeed we can, kind sir!' Bonaparte was gobbling stew. 'A secret shared is a secret halved! In faith, I shall tell no one who is not interested.'

'They got rid of me,' Lionel whispered. 'Orders from the *highest possible* source, if you know what I mean.' He tapped his nose. 'Well, they claimed the pressure of work was getting to me. But I know the real reason. They'd wanted to silence me for months, ever since I first got close to the truth about Chunky's Chocolate Factory testing their dangerous chemicals on unknowing humans with the Double Chocolate, Triple Marshmallow, Quadruple Crunchy Fudge No-Fat, No-Cholesterol, No-Dairy Chocolate Bar.'

Eddy felt she ought to say something. 'That does sound suspicious.'

'Sounds downright disgusting, if you ask me,' Augustus said.

'That was just the beginning!' Lionel continued. 'Once you scratch the surface, there are cover-ups and corruption lurking everywhere. But no, no, they wouldn't listen to me about Chunky's. They didn't listen to me about the "boy bands" either, but when I found out the Chief Inspector was really a six-foot bearded woman called Mabel, I refused to be silenced any longer. I tried to unmask him when he gave his opening speech at the Annual Police Chiefs' Conference, but his beard wouldn't come off, however hard I pulled. Well, next thing you know, I'm fired! Chief Inspector knew I'd got too close to his dark secret.'

Eddy choked on a mouthful of stew. 'Unbelievable . . .' she said. This strange man was terribly kind, but the warmth of the fire was seeping into her icy bones, and she longed to curl up and drift off to sleep.

'I went quietly, of course. Didn't want them to press charges. Besides –' he lowered his voice to a whisper again – 'I already had other concerns on the back-burner . . .' He jerked his head in the direction of the retirement home. 'But that can wait. You must tell me *everything* you know about Leviticus. What did you see? What did you hear?' He seized a messy notepad from underneath the pot of stew and poised himself to scribble in it. 'And how did you escape? Did you flee down a secret passage? There *has* to be a secret passage.'

'Er . . . not exactly.' Eddy kicked Bonaparte, who was gasping with excitement at the very thought. 'We just slid down the banisters, fell into a big dustcart and got wheeled away.'

'Perhaps,' Bonaparte had not been silenced by the kick, 'we were wheeled away *down a secret passage*! What thinkest thou, Mr Lionel?'

'I think that's a distinct possibility,' Lionel said.

Eddy was glad that the doorbell rang at that moment, which masked Augustus's snort of derision.

Lionel sprang to his feet like an arthritic panther. 'Stay here and stay quiet,' he hissed. 'Someone may have followed you. I'll get rid of them.'

Eddy held her breath as she heard Lionel open the front door.

'. . . No, I haven't got a room for the night. What do you think this is, a hotel?'

She could breathe again. It was just some poor soul attracted by the guest-house sign.

'. . . I have to find somewhere to sleep! Are there no hotels around here?'

'. . . Read the sign next time!' came Lionel's reply as he slammed the door. 'Honestly,' he said as he came back into the living room, bringing the freezing outside air with him. 'You'd think people would get the message. Funny-looking woman too. Who on earth wears sunglasses in the middle of the night? Now . . .' He turned a page in his notebook. 'This secret passage you were telling me about.'

'I'm sure Avril would be able to tell you lots about Leviticus,' Eddy said. 'Secret passages and all. But we don't know where she is.'

'And who is this Avril?'

'Dr Avril Crump. She rescued us from the laboratory after the explosion . . .'

'Laboratory . . . explosion . . .' Lionel scribbled in his notebook.

'We really need her help. She's the only one who

knows about us, apart from the man who wants to kill us. And she's the only friend we've got.'

'You've got me too,' Lionel said.

Eddy's throat thickened. 'Thank you, Lionel. Maybe you can help us find her. She lives in this town.'

'Well, I'll do all I can. Did this Avril mention anywhere in particular?'

Eddy was thinking hard, casting her tired mind back to the meeting in the broom cupboard. 'No . . .' she said. 'Although . . .'

'Yes?'

'Well, I was just remembering that Avril did mention some*one* in particular. The man who created us. A Professor Blot, or something. Perhaps he might be able to help us.'

'Professor Blot,' Lionel said, writing down the name. 'That rings a bell. Tell you what, I'll go to the library first thing in the morning and see what information I can find on the Web.'

'*Web?*' Bonaparte shrieked, clutching his legs up to his chest. 'I am afeard of spiders!'

'World Wide Web,' Lionel explained. 'The Internet? Well, I suppose if you've only got long-dead people's DNA, you wouldn't know anything about stuff like the Internet.'

'*I* know . . .' Eddy hesitated and screwed up her eyes. 'I think I know . . . The Internet . . . It's familiar . . .'

'Well, maybe you've got some other DNA too . . .' But, bright-eyed and alert, Lionel was too excited about secret tunnels to dwell on the clones' specific DNA. 'Now, tell me more about your escape . . .'

Augustus raised a paw.

'Yes?' Lionel was poised with his notebook.

'Throw another log on the fire,' said the dog, settling down for a long and comfortable doze.

8

Morning Has Broken

Dr Sedukta awoke as Wretchford Church's dismal bell chimed four. She shifted uncomfortably on her bench. In the harsh electric glare of the lights from the nearby high street, Memorial Park was not a nice place to sleep on a freezing winter night. Avoiding a particularly splintery patch on the bench, she curled her legs up tight and pulled her thin labcoat closer around her shuddering shoulders. She was not accustomed to spending nights out in the open. Her jobs usually took her to the best hotels in the most glamorous locations in the world, not park benches in horrible little towns like this. Only one guesthouse in the place, and that miserable old man wouldn't even let her in!

A bitter gust of wind suddenly rolled across the

park, gathering speed and almost knocking her off the bench. Her legs, numb with cold, trailed uselessly on the ground. She hauled herself up into a sitting position and stared out into the night with stinging eyes.

She could give up now. There was bound to be a taxi-cab somewhere in the town, and she could be on the road to civilisation instead of shivering on this bench. Then an aeroplane out to somewhere exotic and far away. But if she abandoned this job, her boss would hunt her down to the furthest corners of the globe. There was nowhere to hide from a man like him.

Dr Sedukta shuddered again, but not because of the cold. *She simply had to find the clones.* And if she did not, it would be better to freeze to death than endure the dreadful punishment that failure would certainly entail.

She took out her mobile phone and tapped in a number with a trembling fingernail.

'I thought I should keep you updated,' she said. 'I'm in Wretchford-on-the-Reeke. They'll be here looking for April Crump, I'm sure of it. As soon as I find them, I'll deliver them to you.'

'*Do so.*'

The phone went dead.

Dr Sedukta replaced the phone in her pocket and

turned back to her wooden bench to lie down again. A small pigeon had landed where her head had been, and was hunched up against the cold.

'Hello, little bird,' crooned Dr Sedukta. 'Sleeping in my space, are you?'

She reached out a hand and snapped the pigeon's neck. Then she brushed its still-warm body on to the ground and lay back on the bench.

She needed more sleep. It was going to be a very busy day.

It was half past five in the morning when Lionel parked his yellow Mini on the deserted high street outside Wretchford Town Library. Pleasantly soothed by the stew, the three clones had dropped off to sleep beside the fire one by one. Eddy had told Lionel as much as she knew about the contents of the dustcart, which for some reason he was particularly interested in, until her eyelids drooped, and a welcome wave of wooziness washed over her weary body. Lionel had covered her with a blanket and promised he would be back soon.

Lionel had not been a policeman for so long without picking up a few handy tips from house burglars, and he was well used to sneaking into the library in the dead of night. It was the only time he could go and use the Internet without being thrown out by the librarian, who had banned him several years previously for causing a nuisance. He opened up his car boot and took out a metal crowbar, then padded silently across the frozen pavement and round to the back of the library. There was the large, low window he usually used. It only took a moment to jemmy it open with his crowbar, and slightly longer to haul himself through. It got more difficult every time, and Lionel paused for a moment to rest his aching limbs. But there wasn't a moment to waste.

He felt his way through the darkened hallways to the small computer room and settled at the terminal. Logging on to the Internet, he spent a happy few minutes glancing through his favourite websites – extremelysuspiciouscoverups.com, and unlikelycoincidencesthatshooktheworld.co.uk – before remembering that there was work to be done.

He tapped Professor Blot's name into a search engine.

Your search – Professor Blot – did not match any documents. Do you mean Professor Blut*?*

'Er . . . I suppose I might,' Lionel said, clicking on the alternative spelling.

Professor Gideon Blut . . . Rogue scientist expelled from top laboratory for illicit human cloning.

Lionel's heart did a little leap. He entered the page to read the article in full.

Body parts found in basement . . . developed new technology . . . no comment from Leviticus . . .

Lionel could hardly believe this was happening. He had never managed to get information like this on the Chunky's scandal! He took out his notebook and began scribbling away.

Eddy dozed until just after seven o'clock in the morning, when she was awoken by her own shivering. Lionel's fire had burned itself out, and the coals were chill and grey. Neither Augustus nor Bonaparte was to be seen, but there were loud noises coming from the kitchen. Rubbing her hands together for warmth, Eddy got up and peered round into the kitchen. It did not look like it had the night before. Bonaparte was there, humming a tune, and barely visible behind a mist of washing-up-liquid bubbles. He brandished a small mop. Every surface gleamed.

'Good morrow!' he beamed. 'Stew?'

'Er . . .'

''Twill be a tasty meal, Miss Eddy! I have done

away with the moulds, the infestations and the small plague of mice that did conceal themselves in the biscuit barrel.'

Eddy began to feel queasy.

'And I have made many a fascinating discovery. This jug, for example –' he picked up the kettle – 'doth boil water with no more than the flick of yon switch! And yon mysterious container –' the toaster – 'who knows what magic *this* may perform? *I* suspect it to be a device in which sausages may be toasted. Oh, Miss Eddy! I shall toast sausages for dear Lady Avril when once again we find her! She doth look as though she may be partial to a toasted sausage.'

'That's wonderful, Bony.' Eddy patted him on the shoulder.

'And, Miss Eddy . . .' Bonaparte was turning slightly pink. 'I have also a surprise in store for the marvellous Mr Dog.' He reached under his hat and took out a bundle of paper. 'Might I be permitted to demonstrate it to thee?'

'Well, yes, Bony, but it rather depends what it . . .'

''Tis a song!' Bonaparte waved the pages at her. 'I have been working upon it in my head for some time, and inscribed it upon these sheets whilst thou did sleep. 'Tis entitled "My Name is Mr Dog". A good title, think ye not?'

'Well, I suppose . . .'

'Good friends, I prithee, gather round me
and hear my tale – it will astound thee.
'Tis but one day since Mother Earth
was blessed by heaven with my birth,
the which was so unorthodox
that, verily, 'twill blow thy socks.
Prepare to find thyselves amazed
and marvel at the issues raised
and learn enthralled, entranced, agog,
the wondrous tale of Mr Dog.
For yea, my name is Mr Dog!
Hooray, my name is Mr Dog!
All say, my name is Mr Dog!
My name is Mr Dog.'

Bonaparte's hand, which had been thumping the table rhythmically, hovered in mid-air. He beamed at his one-person audience.

'There are several more verses to be enjoyed, Miss Eddy, and thou art warmly invited to join in with yon chorus.'

'Er . . . thank you, Bony, but not now.' Eddy was already backing towards the door at speed. 'I really *must* go and wake Augustus. Lionel may be back with information any minute now. Tell you what, why don't you make us all a hot cup of tea?'

'But of course!' Bonaparte seized the kettle. 'What with this miraculous jug, we shall partake of tea in no time at all. There will be time a-plenty for song.' He pulled open the fridge and gasped. 'A chilled cabinet! ''Tis a home fit for a king!'

Bonaparte's strange ditty rang in Eddy's ears as she escaped to look for Augustus. Suspecting where the dog might be, she marched up the stairs and tried the first door on the left. Sure enough, it was a bedroom. And sure enough, Augustus was there.

He was standing in front of a full-length mirror, contorting himself into a ridiculous pose and pouting slightly as he admired his reflection.

'Sleep well?'

Thinking fast, Augustus crumpled to the floor. 'Where am I?' he gasped. '*Who* am I?' he added, twitching and looking wild. 'I must be delirious! The cold last night . . . I have a terrible fever . . .'

'Come on.' Eddy grinned. 'We haven't got time to be delirious. We should get ready. We may need to leave quickly when Lionel gets back.'

Bonaparte's voice floated upstairs. 'Breakfast, Mr Dog? I am making the most delicious stew!'

'Is he *completely* insane?' Augustus snapped. 'I don't want stew for *breakfast*. It's bad enough for dinner. Can't he serve something more suitable for a dog?'

'I have some lovely fresh carrots,' Bonaparte was calling, 'and a delicious piece of meat. I did also take some ripe tomatoes and juicy mushrooms. 'Twill be a veritable feast!'

'Really, Bony, we don't have time for . . .'

Eddy paused. Then she went to the door and peered down the stairs.

'What do you mean, you *took* some tomatoes? Where did you take them from?'

'Oh, Miss Eddy, 'twas a wonderful place. All manner of comestibles did adorn the shelves! Women did fill rolling carts with a marvellous array of goods. There were fruits there I could never have dreamed of! And meat – oh, what meat! – in perfect little packages!'

'Bony,' Eddy said. 'You went out? Alone? *Shopping?*'

'The institution proclaimed itself to be a supermarket,' Bonaparte continued, 'but *I* would not stop at such modesty. 'Twas more than super – 'twas a *splendid* market.'

'How did you *pay* for this food?' Eddy was fierce as she came down the stairs.

'*Pay?*' echoed Bonaparte. 'But I did not think . . .'

The doorbell rang.

'Visitors!' Bonaparte shrieked. 'And just in time for song and breakfast!'

He bounded for the door. Thinking fast, Eddy stuck out a foot.

'No!' she hissed as he gazed up at her from the floor. 'Don't answer it! Just stay quiet and they might go away.'

The doorbell rang again, longer this time.

Eddy shook her head as Bonaparte opened his mouth. 'Don't even think about it. They'll go away in a min –'

There was a pounding on the door.

'Police! Open up!'

'Police!' Bonaparte looked thrilled. 'They must be friends of dear Mr Lionel! We must invite them in!'

'No!' Eddy said. 'Don't move.' She tried to stay calm and think. Lulled into a false sense of security while Lionel had been around, she was back on full alert. She could not let the police into the house. Bonaparte was far too much of a liability.

'Hey! Eddy! What's all the racket? Can't a dog get any peace around here?'

Oh, and there was the small matter of the talking dog at the top of the stairs. Eddy turned to face him.

'Go and hide in the bedroom! You too, Bony.' She hauled Bonaparte to his feet and gave him a shove up the stairs. 'Do *not* come out until I say so.'

'Bossy Boots,' Augustus grumbled. 'Do this, do that, go here, go there . . .' He pulled Bonaparte up the last few stairs towards him with his teeth. 'This wouldn't happen in Japan, you know. People talking to the emperor's guard dog in your tone would be fed to the lions. Or *worse*.'

'Just do what I say –' Eddy eyed Augustus – 'and button it.'

Sulking now, Augustus stalked back to the bedroom. Eddy took a deep breath, composed her features into an innocent smile and opened the door. A uniformed policeman, in mid-bang, fell forward and landed with a yelp.

'Good morning,' Eddy said. 'Can I help you?'

Another dark blue figure, a scowling policewoman, looked down at her. 'Get up, Watts,' she said, without taking her eyes off Eddy. 'May we speak to your father, dear?'

'My father?' Eddy shuffled forward and carefully pulled the door to behind her. Net curtains were twitching all along the street as nosy neighbours spotted the police car.

'A man was seen entering this house after stealing eighteen pounds and seventy-one pence worth of goods from the twenty-four hour branch of Sunny's Supermarkets on Reeke Way. Tall, very thin. Is that your dad?'

'No, I'm afraid it isn't.' Eddy smiled again.

The policewoman's beady eyes narrowed. 'Let us in, dear.' It did not sound as if she thought Eddy was very dear at all.

'I'm sorry. I'm not allowed to talk to strangers.'

'Right.' The policewoman gave up all pretence of kindness. 'Watts, search the house.'

'Shall I break the door down again?' Watts said.

'Yes, if necessary,' the policewoman said. 'I want this place turned upside down.'

Eddy's brain was working very fast. 'There's no one here but me! I'm all alone. I'm . . . er . . .'

'An orphan?' Watts gazed down at her sadly.

'Yes!' Eddy beamed at him. 'Yes, an orphan! That's

it. It's very sad,' she said, wobbling her lower lip. 'I shouldn't have done it. But I was hungry. Er . . . I didn't dare do the shoplifting myself,' she continued, 'so I found an old tramp to do it for me.'

'*An old tramp?*'

'Yes – a complete stranger. He got me the food, and then he vanished. I think he went that way.' She gestured vaguely down the road. 'I'm sorry. I was starving.'

There was silence for a moment, broken only by the sound of the policeman sniffling.

'Watts!' snapped the policewoman. 'For heaven's sake, pull yourself together.' She glared down at Eddy. 'Is this the truth?'

'Why would I lie?' Eddy said. 'My dear, dead parents taught me *never* to lie.'

Watts began to sob. 'Poor little mite . . .'

'All right.' The policewoman looked at Watts with disgust. 'We'll have to believe you. But we shall be looking for this tramp. We can't have his sort corrupting children. Now, you'd better come along with us.'

Eddy stared at her.

'What do you mean?'

'We can't leave you here all alone. Look at you – dressed in that thin little white coat – in *this* weather! It's amazing Social Services haven't done anything.' The policewoman took Eddy's arm.

Eddy wriggled in her grasp. 'You can't take me away!' She appealed to the tearful Watts for help. 'Please! I'm not an orphan! It *was* all a lie. My uncle Lionel has just gone out for a few minutes. I can't leave . . .'

Watts patted her head. 'I understand. A fantasy world must be very appealing. But your parents would have wanted the best for you. Your school work must be suffering.'

'School?' Eddy repeated blankly.

'You do *go* to school?' demanded the policewoman. Eddy's terrified stare was her only response. 'Delinquent,' she muttered. 'Well, you *will* go to school. Starting today. And just to make sure you don't wheedle your way out of it, we'll take you there ourselves, after we've seen Social Services.' She dragged Eddy down the icy garden path and pushed her into the car. The door slammed shut.

Eddy felt sick with fear as she stared up at the house. There was a furry face at the window, all hint of its usual smirk gone.

'YOU'VE BEEN SO KIND!' she suddenly howled, at the top of her lungs. 'TAKING ME TO

SCHOOL AND EVERYTHING. I'M SURE I'LL LOVE IT.' She prayed that Augustus could hear her. 'Tell me,' she lowered her voice to speak to Watts, 'is school far away?'

'We'll probably take you to St Swithin's. It's only round the corner.'

Eddy wound down her window. 'I CAN HARDLY WAIT!' she roared. *'ST SWITHIN'S* SCHOOL! AND ONLY *ROUND THE CORNER* TOO!'

As the car began to pull away, she saw Augustus nod.

'She's clearly disturbed,' she overheard Watts say to the policewoman.

'Either that or just plain loopy.'

But Eddy did not care what the policewoman thought. Augustus had heard her cries. Lionel would know where she had been taken. It was the best she could do for now.

9

The Black Sheep of Leviticus

The first thing Avril realised as she awoke from her long, unnatural sleep was that she was alone. There was no sign of Dr Wetherby. This could only be a good thing.

Even better was the soft suede of the sofa on which she found herself sitting. It was the colour of pale buttermilk, and as strokeable as a baby's skin. It felt wonderful. She wriggled luxuriously for a few moments before noticing that her elbows, grimy with soot from the explosion, had left a dirty mark. The fabric was so delicate that a bit of spit-and-polish only made it worse. Avril placed a strategic cushion over the grey patch, hopped to her feet and looked around.

She was standing, grubbily and shabbily, in the most magnificent room she had ever seen. Tall bookshelves towered from the rich wooden floor to the high-vaulted ceiling. They were filled with leather-bound, gold-embossed books. Glossy oil paintings hung in the spaces between the bookshelves. Antique tables were elegantly decorated with exquisite lamps and ornamental curiosities. A fire that was far too tasteful to roar or crackle simply glowed warmly in a moulded fireplace. It was beautiful.

In a bit of a daze, and grinding grit from her shoes into the thick rugs, Avril wandered towards the only visible door. She tried the brass handle. It was locked tight. So she was a prisoner. Cream suede sofas and glowing log fires were all very well, but Avril needed to be out there searching for the clones. Dr Wetherby might have caught up with them by now.

Then she saw it.

The tea tray. There it sat, on the large desk. An enormous silver tray, laden with teapot, cups, saucers and plates. Plates that were piled high with sandwiches and scones. There were little sponge cakes with pink icing. There were large sponge cakes with green icing. There were sticky buns, there were chocolate éclairs, there were huge blueberry muffins. *There were doughnuts.*

Avril's stomach rumbled.

'No!' she said to herself. 'This is no time for

snacks! You've got friends to save!'

She turned her back on the tea tray and began pulling out books from the tall shelves, hoping that one of them might conceal a mechanism to some sort of secret passage. She had not watched all those action films for nothing. The floor was covered with books by the time she gave up and decided to try something else. She started tapping along the dark wooden panelling down one side of the room, listening for any hollow sounds. When this too led to nothing, Avril threw back one of the thick rugs and scanned the parquet floor for gaps before digging her short fingernails into the thin lines between floorboards. She strained and heaved, but the floor stayed put.

Wiping the sweat from her forehead, Avril stood up and scanned the room for another escape possibility. Locked door, solid floorboards, no secret passages . . . She was panting heavily, as much from anxiety as from exertion. Her eyes alighted again on the silver tray as steam curled from the teapot.

'Perhaps just one cup . . .' Her stomach rumbled again, louder this time. 'If I'm going to find those clones,' Avril decided, 'I'll need my strength. And I can take supplies . . .'

She poured a cup of boiling tea and drank deep,

then took a piece of fruit cake and ate it hungrily. Now for those supplies . . . What would the clones want to eat when she found them? She had just popped an enormous jam doughnut into the pocket of her labcoat when she heard a noise at the door. Somebody was coming in. She tried hurriedly to swallow the large, partially chewed chunk of fruit cake. A currant went down the wrong way. She choked noisily.

'Dr Crump?' The door clicked almost silently shut. 'Are you quite all right?'

Avril spluttered cake crumbs all over the shining floor.

'That looked rather uncomfortable. I'm afraid I have startled you.'

The words seemed friendly enough; the male voice was smooth and mellifluous. But Avril was on her guard. She pulled herself together, looked up, and blinked. Then a hot blush began to spread over her face.

He was the best-looking man she had ever seen.

'I do apologise for the manner of your arrival last night, Dr Crump. I do not like to drug my guests. But security is of the utmost importance. Ah, I see you have made a start on the refreshments. I do like a woman with a healthy appetite.' He raked a hand through his thick blond hair and smiled again. His teeth were beautifully white. They matched his pristine labcoat.

'You're a *scientist*?' Avril stared at his broad shoulders and ocean-green eyes.

'Indeed I am.' He tilted his head, displaying a strong jaw.

Avril giggled girlishly. Then hiccuped.

'Welcome to Gargoyle Manor, Dr Crump.' The vision moved towards the cream suede sofa and lowered himself on to it. He patted the other end of the sofa. 'Please, sit down.'

Avril was not too dazzled by her visitor to remember that an ugly grey stain covered the patch beneath the cushion. She sat hurriedly, before he could lift it.

'I hope you have been comfortable in my library, Dr Crump – or may I call you April?' He put his hand on her knee and squeezed it gently. He was wearing an elegant silver signet ring. 'This is my favourite room in Gargoyle Manor. The previous owner, the thirty-fourth Earl of Midden, let it fall into terrible disrepair. I only bought the place because it is near Leviticus. After all, what scientist would not wish to be close to the very hub of the scientific world?'

Avril gulped and stared at the hand on her knee. 'Actually, it's Avril,' she murmured. 'But you can call me April if you like!' She was hoping that her bald head was not shining too brightly under the lights.

A brief spasm of irritation passed across the man's handsome face. He drew a black leather notebook from his labcoat pocket and flicked over a few pages. '*Avril* . . .' he muttered. He crossed something out with a small pen and wrote in a few words. His face cleared. 'Forgive me,' he smiled. 'My intelligence sources have let me down. *My* name is Professor Gideon Blut.' He placed his elegant hand back on Avril's knee. '*Please* call me Gideon.'

'Professor Blut?' Avril stared. '*The* Professor Blut?'

'The black sheep of Leviticus Laboratories? The very same, although those who worked with me back then would not recognise me now. My appearance has – shall we say – improved somewhat these last fifteen years.' He closed his eyes for a moment and raised his head, as though basking in sunlight. 'Do you think me handsome, Avril?'

'Oh, *yes*! I mean . . . yes . . . I do . . . very handsome. Very handsome indeed . . .'

'Very handsome indeed . . .' Gideon's eyes flicked open. 'Just as I was always *meant to be*. Nature likes its little jokes, Avril. You of all people will know what I mean.' He smiled and gave Avril's bald head a gentle pat. 'Nature tries to spread out the power. Those who are beautiful are not permitted to be intelligent. Those who are ugly –' he gave a bitter little laugh – 'are dealt the consolation of a fine mind. But I play with Nature, Avril. I see no reason why a genius – like myself – cannot also be pleasing to the eye. Do you?'

Avril squeaked.

'Tell me, how *are* things at Leviticus?'

'Well, I –'

'*I* have prospered since those wretches threw me out in ignominy,' Gideon interrupted. 'Of course, they would no doubt condemn my work – fools often condemn that which they do not understand. 'But as you see –' he gestured at the opulent library, then turned to her with a dazzling smile – 'disgrace has its rewards. You and I are mavericks, Avril. We do not need the approval of those we despise. I cannot wait to see the faces of all those who mocked and belittled me over the years when they discover how I have thrived!'

Avril yelped as his hand gave her knee another gentle squeeze. The silver ring he wore was decorated with some sort of insignia. It looked rather like a large bird about to devour a smaller one. She reached for a sandwich to distract herself.

'But enough of Leviticus.' Gideon leaned in

conspiratorially. 'I want to tell you about my new work. My Mission.'

'Mission . . .?' Avril was starting to feel rather giddy in his presence.

Gideon poured himself a cup of tea and took a sip. 'It has been my dream, ever since I started my revolutionary research into human cloning all those years ago at Leviticus, to create a world governed solely by the principles of Blut's Law.'

'Blut's Law?'

'Yes . . .' Gideon gave her a perplexed glance. 'Do you *always* repeat everything people say, Avril? It's an extremely tiresome habit, if I may say so. Please do not interrupt my train of thought again.' He sat back and sipped his tea. 'Blut's Law: *Human success is inversely proportional to human degeneracy*. Not widely known yet in scientific circles – or in *any* circles!' He chuckled at his own joke. 'But that will not be the case for much longer.'

'Human degeneracy . . .?'

'Is there an echo in here, do you think, Avril?' Sitting up straight now, Gideon's green eyes were flints of steel. 'Or are you simply ignoring my *polite request* that you refrain from repeating my every word?'

'Oh, no, no . . .' Avril preferred it when his eyes

were gazing benevolently at her. 'It's just that I don't understand . . . Blut's Law . . .'

Once again, Gideon flicked open his notebook, studying a page in puzzlement. 'Yes,' he murmured to himself, 'it *does* say here that she's highly intelligent . . .' He looked up at Avril again, and this time spoke very loudly and clearly: 'HUMAN . . . SUCCESS . . . IS . . . INVERSELY . . . PROPORTIONAL . . . TO . . . HUMAN . . . DEGENERACY. In other words – in *simpler* words, if you prefer – it is time to skim off the scum and start again. Let me tell you a little story, Avril, about how Blut's Law began. Do stop me if you're not following.' He sipped his tea. 'Not long after I had begun working with that second-rate cell cloning team at Leviticus, a starving beggar approached me as I was leaving my house one morning. He was a filthy, smelly old man, covered in sores and boils, and dressed in appalling rags. He was ill with a cancer, he said, and horribly frostbitten from spending nights on the street. It was *then* that I had my beautiful moment of inspiration, Avril!'

'To find a cure for his cancer!' Avril felt relief sweep over her. She had obviously misunderstood him, what with that rather alarming talk of missions and degeneracy. 'To find a scientific solution to world hunger . . .'

Gideon smiled at her, and patted her hand. 'Dear Lord, no. To destroy him.'

Avril's delicious sandwich – moist smoked salmon and soft brown bread – suddenly tasted of cardboard. She choked.

'Him, and all his kind. All the losers, Avril. All the good-for-nothings.' He leaned forward, his green eyes glowing, not looking at Avril but gazing into space. 'I can do it! I can create a race of super-beings! I can rid the world of the cripples, the deformed, the *stupid* –' he raised an eyebrow in her direction – 'the old, the infirm, the weak, the very *dregs* –' his lip curled – 'of this failing society. I call them NVs, Avril – the Non-Viables. Just imagine how beautiful this world will be without them. Think of what can be achieved when the human race is cleansed of undesirables and filled with the *very best* that my unique cloning technology can offer!'

Avril could not quite believe what she was hearing. She even glanced over her shoulder for a moment, hopeful that she might see the Leviticus staff gathered behind, reeling with gales of laughter at this joke at her expense. But nobody was there, and the cruel twist to

Gideon's lips that she had suddenly noticed left her in no doubt that he was telling the truth. 'But *why*?' was all she could manage.

'Well, why *not*?' Gideon sat back again and roared with laughter at his wit. 'Tell me, why *not*, Avril?' he said, when he had recovered. 'Why *not* push back the boundaries, why *not* take science beyond its limits? The ones with the knowledge are scared of the possibilities! Most scientists will only go so far. Cowards! Cloning sheep, and pigs . . .' Gideon sneered. 'Don't make me laugh! And as for *talking dogs*, the very idea disgusts me.'

Avril opened her mouth. A remnant of sandwich fell out. 'But . . . but . . . how do you know about that . . .?' Now she was booming again, her nerves playing havoc with her already-peculiar voice.

'I have . . . how shall I put it . . . an *associate* in place at Leviticus Laboratories. I think you may know her – Dr Sedukta.'

'Dr Sedukta,' Avril repeated faintly.

'Of course, she's only been employed there a short time, but before I am done, she will have informed me of every single one of Leviticus's scientific secrets. She has already proved her worth by bringing your talents to my attention, and by telling me about your . . . little accident. I must confess that it never occurred to me that anyone would attempt to use my old equipment – especially not a clumsy prototype like the Mark One. I should have been *much* more careful . . .' His face darkened for a moment, and he chewed the side of an elegant finger. 'No matter,' he murmured to himself, 'it can still be cleared up . . .' He shook himself and smiled down at Avril again. 'Dr Sedukta is hunting down the filthy mongrel clones even as we speak. More tea?' He did not wait for a reply before pouring her a cup.

Avril was feeling very sick. 'She isn't going to . . . *kill* them, is she?'

'Oh, no, no, no!' Gideon looked horrified at this suggestion.

'Thank God!' Avril almost collapsed with relief.

'No,' Gideon continued, 'Dr Sedukta's preferred methods of killing are *far* too specialised to waste on Non-Viables. Expensive, too. Once she has tracked them down, her job is over. I have plenty of other staff to take care of disposal. Now –' he leaned forward as Avril shrank back, whimpering – 'could you tell me if Dr Sedukta has at least one fact correct? Is there a little girl amongst your three NVs? Almost normal-looking?'

'Oh, no,' Avril whispered. 'Please don't hurt Edna.'

'*Edna.*' Gideon made a note. 'Excellent! Thank you, Avril. I'm sure you are as excited about the prospect of experimenting on her as I am. I am hopeful that her brain will provide some extremely valuable insights! I'm looking forward to having the chance to dissect it and examine it at first hand in the Medical Centre . . . The other two NVs,' he said, waving a dismissive hand, 'will just go direct to Room 237, out in the woods.'

'W-what's in Room 237?'

'Ah,' Gideon smiled. 'That is something I could only tell you if you were to agree to come and work for me, dear Avril.'

'Work for you?' Avril gazed at him in horror. 'What on earth do you mean?'

'Thanks to your accident up in Lab One, you know a great deal more about the progress of human cloning than is desirable. But you are – apparently – a brilliant scientist, Avril. Misguided, perhaps: Dr Sedukta has informed me about your mop research, but we need never mention that again. I want people like you on my team. Your new knowledge is not necessarily a problem – *if you use it in the right way*. Does it not excite you?' He was watching her closely. 'My technology puts us decades ahead of all those other dullards who tinker with cloning, Avril. We are very close to creating the perfect being. We are only a hair's breadth away. You could be a part of the Mission! Of course, if you refuse, it puts me in a very difficult position . . .' His hand slid back on to her knee. '*Join us,*' he hissed. 'You must see, Avril, that you are either with me or against me.'

Avril found some strength in her trembling legs. She leapt up, showering tea over cream suede. 'I don't want to create a new race! It's evil!'

Gideon's eyes widened. 'Evil?' he repeated softly.

'I'll never work for you! It's vile! You're a lunatic.'

Gideon put his head on one side and regarded Avril thoughtfully. 'Oh dear,' he said. 'Oh *dear.* This is most unfortunate, *Dr Crump.* I really had hoped that you could be a valuable part of my team. Clearly –' he took a long pause – 'for the first time in my life –' another pause – 'I was wrong.'

'Look, just let me go!' Avril was very frightened now. 'I won't tell the police. Just let me go and we can all stay out of each other's way.'

A smile spread once more across his handsome face. This time it contorted his features. 'You fool,' he said quietly. '*Let you go?* After what you've been told? Oh, I think that's very unlikely, don't you?' Suddenly

Gideon sprang to his feet, towering over Avril. His whole face had been transformed now. His lips were drawn back, baring his teeth, and his green eyes were dangerously cold. 'Sit down!'

Avril sat down.

'Let me tell you, it is not *I* who is mad, Dr Crump. It is this foul and filthy world, which refuses to see the way of the future. I had hoped that *you* might see it. Sadly it seems that your use to me is very limited.' He leaned towards her. 'Did you enjoy your tea, Dr Crump?'

Horror was making Avril's eyes bulge. 'Did you put poison in it?' she gasped.

'Now, really, Dr Crump.' Gideon tutted. 'Do you honestly think I would be so crude? And why would I put anything *in* your cup when I can simply take something *off* it?'

In a flash, he pulled a thin pair of tongs and a clear plastic bag from his pocket. Handling the tongs delicately, he picked up Avril's empty teacup and popped it into the bag.

'A saliva sample.' He smiled, though his eyes did not. 'All the better to clone you with, my dear.'

Avril felt her insides wrench. 'You're making a clone of me,' she said. 'To lure the clones to you.'

Tears began to run down her round cheeks. 'Don't do this to us.'

But Gideon was not listening, engrossed in the teacup. 'I'll add a dash of psychopath's DNA,' he mused, 'so that the clone has the requisite depravity . . .'

'The clones will never believe it's really me. They *know* me! I'm their friend!'

Gideon blinked at her. 'If you will excuse me,' he said softly, 'I have work to do.' He reached into the pocket of his pristine white coat and brought out a small walkie-talkie. 'Blut to Security. Blut to Security. Bring the other one to the library.' He replaced the device and smiled at Avril again. 'I think you'll like this, Dr Crump. I have a charming cellmate for you. As soon as Dr Sedukta and your clone return with the NVs, you can *all* pay a little visit to Room 237.'

Avril could hear the various bolts unlocking, followed by a familiar blustering voice as the door opened.

'How dare you treat me like this! This is kidnapping! Don't you know who I am? I'm Deputy Head of Oil and Fuel and Director of Experimental Affairs! I'm a future Governor of Leviticus . . .'

Dr Wetherby and his briefcase were carried in by a thuggish-looking brute with cauliflower ears and dumped unceremoniously on the sofa.

'Dr Wetherby.' Gideon did not smile. 'How . . . *inconsequential* it is to see you again. From what Dr Sedukta has told me, you sound as unutterably tedious as ever.'

Dr Wetherby glared at him. 'Who are *you*?' he demanded.

'You do not recognise me? Well, I have carried out a great deal of experimental work on my own body since those fools at Leviticus thought fit to expel me.'

Dr Wetherby's jaw fell open. '*Blut?*' he gasped. 'But . . . you were shorter . . . *weedier* . . . with all those boils . . . brown teeth . . .'

Gideon flinched. 'Who's to say *you* couldn't use a little improvement?' he hissed, before quickly covering his fury with a ghastly smile. 'Now, the last time I saw you, Wetherby,' he continued, giving Avril a wink, 'you were cheating your way to win Leviticus's Annual General Knowledge Quiz.'

'I never did! I won that fair and square!'

'You're a LIAR!' A vein bulged in Gideon's neck as his head darted towards Wetherby like a cobra's. His smooth good looks were contorted by hatred. 'You won't cheat your way out of *this*, Wetherby!' he screamed. 'I've waited fifteen years to have the satisfaction of revenge on the whole repulsive pack of you! Leviticus will regret the day it angered this sleeping giant! You will all beg for my mercy, but I will be merciless! *Merciless* . . .' He was almost choking, gasping for air, and this forced him to stop. He turned away for a moment, breathing deeply. Then he raked his hands once again through his hair and turned around. Calm once more, he nodded at the brute. 'Lock them in. These two aren't going anywhere.'

He turned on his heel and walked briskly to the door.

'And do not mistake me, Dr Crump. I *will* get them.'

The door shut behind him.

10

School's In

Eddy sat at her desk at the front of the classroom and stared at the floor, trying to keep her head down in more ways than one. From the moment she had arrived at the school gates, she had stuck out thanks to the slime-green uniform she had been given to wear.

It was what they called dress-down day at St Swithin's, and *nobody else* was wearing the uniform.

Frightened as she had been by the arrival of the police, Eddy had got rather excited about this visit to school. As long as Bonaparte and Augustus were safely hidden away, she felt sure she could survive out in the real world for a short time. The kind Social Services lady had treated her just as if she was an ordinary little girl, slipping her a handful of sweets and winking at her sympathetically behind the policewoman's back.

As Watts had driven her towards St Swithin's, passing gangs of children with footballs and backpacks, she had entertained a fleeting hope that she might even make some friends.

But things were not working out very well. Now, as she absorbed herself in the brown patch in front of her feet, she could feel twenty-five pairs of eyes boring into the back of her head.

'Who's the freak in green?' one girl sniggered. Somebody flicked an elastic band at the back of Eddy's neck and, when she did not respond, followed it up with a sharp pellet of paper. Eddy rubbed her stinging skin and lowered her head further, too bewildered to confront the culprit. Maybe this was what they did in school. She only hoped it did not go on all day.

'What's your name, freak in green?'

'Oh! My name's Eddy.' Eddy turned around, a sudden smile brightening her face, ready to strike up a conversation. 'I . . .'

'Catch!' someone called out, just before she received a shocking thud to the head. A large black-and-white ball bounced away to the front of the classroom. Frightened though she was, Eddy was outraged.

'That hurt!'

'Look! She's even got one eye to match her prissy uniform!'

Eddy gulped and faced the front again. So much for her hopes of fitting in.

The class fell silent for a moment as the door opened. But it was not the teacher, and the noise started up again as a thin, mousy-haired boy crept into the room and slipped into the desk next to Eddy's. He was also wearing the uniform. In fact, he was faring even worse than Eddy thanks to some pebble-thick glasses and a particularly nasty pair of green knee-length shorts.

'New friend for you, Wilfred!' called one of the boys. 'Another creep in a uniform!'

Wilfred did not look up. He too stared at the floor, pushing his glasses up towards the bridge of his nose in a repeated gesture.

Eddy ignored the noise behind her and leaned towards Wilfred.

'Erm . . . hello,' she said. 'I . . . er . . . I'm Eddy. Nice to meet you.'

Wilfred did not reply, slumping down lower in his seat.

'Hey, Freaky Freddy's in luuurve!' squawked a red-haired boy from the far corner. He was a chubby fellow,

again and lowered his voice even further – 'but maybe we could be . . . er . . . friends?'

'*Really?*' Eddy turned to look at Wilfred. 'Wow! Well, I'd really like that!' She felt fizzy with delight, but before she could say any more, the teacher finished her meditation with a swig from a flask and a loud hiccup.

'Now, darlings! I have a very exciting piece of news for you all! Can you guess what it is?'

'You're taking early retirement, Miss Dougall?' someone sniggered.

'Don't be silly, Katie. I'm only thirty-sev . . . twenty-nine. No, I want to talk about the class musical.'

There was a collective groan.

'We have a dilemma on our hands. Our world premiere of my musical version of *Dick Whittington and His Cat* is on tonight, as you know, and we are still short of an actor to play the Cat! Now, one of you is going to have to volunteer. There aren't any words to learn. Well?' Her eyes scanned the classroom. 'Anyone? Anyone? Who's it going to be?'

Eddy was just scrunching down in her seat to avoid Miss Dougall's stare when she heard a sound from the window.

'*Miss Eddy!*'

It was Bonaparte's voice. There was no mistaking it.

'Miss Eddy! 'Tis us!' There was a loud rapping on the window. The entire class turned to stare.

Eddy scrunched down further in her seat and wished she could just disappear.

'Behold, Miss Eddy! We have brought thee a steaming portion of fresh stew! Mr Dog did think thou mightst be hungry.'

'Who on earth is this?' Miss Dougall floated to the window and banged on it loudly. 'Go away!'

'But, my good lady . . .' From the corner of her eye, Eddy saw Bonaparte disappear briefly in a sweeping bow. His voice was muffled through the window pane. 'We simply wish to provide sustenance for our young friend. We did not know it to be a crime.'

Eddy could hear giggles and whispers, but she no longer had time to be scared of her classmates. She calculated that she had about half a second before Augustus decided to speak up, and she bolted to the window.

'Miss Dougall, this is my uncle and his dog. They're perfectly harmless. They just wanted to pay me a visit on my first day. To bring me luck and everything.'

'Not *luck.*' Bonaparte beamed and waved a huge pan. '*Stew.*'

'You know these people?' Miss Dougall frowned.

'Yes, it's my uncle . . . er . . . Burt.' Eddy glared at Augustus. 'And his dog, Bonzo. I mean Augustus!' she cried, as Augustus opened his mouth to speak. 'Uncle's a bit eccentric, but he wouldn't hurt a fly.'

'Why's he wearing that stupid uniform?' Red Hair was staring at them with disgust.

'It's not a stupid uniform!' Wilfred's eyes grew wide behind his glasses as he suddenly realised that he was on his feet and shouting. 'It's really . . . er . . . cool,' he added, subsiding into his seat with flaming cheeks.

Eddy glared at Red Hair. 'It's an authentic Napoleonic uniform and it's *completely unique.*'

'Aye,' Bonaparte added, remembering what Augustus had said to Avril about his clothes the previous day. 'Get thee a life, young master.' He turned back to Miss Dougall. 'May we come in? I am sure there is stew aplenty for all.'

'I hardly think . . .'

Wearing an expression that Eddy was fairly certain qualified as an evil grin, Augustus's head popped into view. He looked directly at Miss Dougall, put his head on one side and gave a little whimper.

'Oh . . . you're rather sweet, aren't you?' Miss Dougall peered through the glass. She clicked her fingers at Eddy before smiling down at Augustus. 'I think we've just found our new actor . . .'

It did not take long for Eddy to conclude that Miss Dougall was an exceedingly stupid woman. Not only had she written a diabolical musical, she also thought Augustus was wonderful.

'*Such* an intelligent dog! And what an actor! The pathos in his eyes! The emotion in his every entrance and exit! If only he could talk!'

'See,' Augustus whispered to Eddy as he sauntered off the school-hall stage and into the wings to a storm of applause from Miss Dougall. '*Someone* appreciates me.'

'Shut up!' Eddy hissed back. 'If anyone hears you talking, we're finished. And in case you'd forgotten, Bony's a wanted man. We've got to keep a low profile. What were you *thinking*, coming to school like this? You've ruined everything for me, Augustus! I was trying to fit in.'

Augustus yawned. 'You're just jealous because you're backstage and I'm the star. Now, do you mind? I've got work to do.'

'*Work?*'

'I have to find my character.' Augustus sank on to a ramshackle chaise longue. 'It's not easy playing a Cat, you know.'

'Don't see why. You're all *animals*.'

Eddy stamped off into the darkened auditorium, nearly tripping on one of the ridiculous piles of turnips that were part of the scenery. Wilfred waved her over from the front row of chairs.

'Haven't you got a part in the play?' Eddy asked as she sat down.

'My father won't let me appear in plays. He says they're a w-waste of time. He thinks everything's a waste of time apart from maths.' Wilfred's voice was deliberately casual as he busied himself with his Props List. 'He makes me d-do maths in the summer holidays. It's my best subject now, but it just makes the others all hate me.'

'What about your mum?'

'She ran off to join the circus. She's a lion-tamer now.'

'A *lion-tamer*?'

Wilfred shrugged. 'She said it would be relaxing compared to living with my d-dad. I get the occasional postcard.'

'Wilfred, are you *sure* you want to be my friend? I mean, I don't want them to pick on you because of me – saying I'm your *girlfriend* and all that rubbish . . .'

'*Fre-ddy and E-ddy,*' Wilfred sang, and grinned at her for the first time, his smile very wide and goofy. 'It's no w-worse than any of the other stuff they say. And I've always wanted a friend. I even used to w-wish I could swap my d-dad for one.'

'He can't be that bad,' Eddy said. 'At least you've *got* a dad. Someone to tell you what to do. Someone to take care of you and make you feel wanted.'

Wilfred blinked at her through his shiny lenses. 'Don't you *have* parents, Eddy?'

'Not exactly,' she said, and for a moment she could see Avril's smiling face. 'Not parents. I had *someone*. But I've lost her.'

'Well,' Wilfred said, 'I think you're lucky with just your uncle and his d-dog.'

Suddenly, Eddy wanted to tell him everything. 'Wilfred, can you keep a secret?'

'A *secret*? Of course I . . .'

'Miss Eddy!' Bonaparte cried, sinking into the seat beside her. 'I am all a-tremble! Mistress Dougall hath commanded me to appear in the play!'

Eddy buried her face in her hands. 'Bony, no!'

'She did think I would make a convincing elderly toothless yokel. And Miss Eddy, I even have yon line to speak: *Oo-ar*.' He tried it out again, with more vigour. '*Oo-arrr*.'

'But . . .'

There was suddenly a loud exclamation from the front of the hall.

'This won't do *at all*!' It was Miss Dougall, staring up at the stage, where the children playing Country Bumpkins hung about picking their noses and scowling. 'Something is missing . . . Augustus! Where are you, precious?'

Augustus smiled down at Eddy as he sauntered onstage.

'PROPS! We need something for dear Augustus to make a big entrance in. Perhaps some sort of chariot . . .' Eddy saw Augustus's eyes light up as Miss Dougall gazed into the distance. '. . . a solo spotlight following him, Bumpkins cheering –'

'I'll make a chariot,' Wilfred interrupted excitedly. 'Me and Eddy can do it this afternoon.'

'We *can*?'

'I'm going to d-design racing-cars when I'm older,' he whispered, pushing his glasses up his nose. 'Making a chariot will be a piece of cake.'

'Thank you, Wilfred,' said Miss Dougall, just as the lunch bell rang. She blew a kiss at Augustus and then, above the noise of stampeding Bumpkins, she called to Wilfred and Eddy. 'Follow me! I'm sure you two can cobble together a sweet little chariot out of some old roller-skates and a cardboard box or two. Bit of gilt paint, that sort of thing.'

Wilfred turned to Eddy. 'Coming?'

'You go on. I'll catch up with you.' Then she was alone with Augustus and Bonaparte.

Augustus glared at her. 'I don't want a chariot made out of spare wheels and grotty cardboard! I shall be giving *serious* consideration to the matter of my continued presence in this play.'

'Oh, Mr Dog, dost thou think, perchance, that *I* could rewrite the scene to thy satisfaction?'

'Look, you two,' Eddy snapped, 'you're not even going to be in this stupid play. Lionel is going to arrive any minute. Then we'll be out of here.' Otherwise, she thought, we're in real trouble . . .

11

Cellmates

Five minutes into her enforced room-share with Dr Wetherby, Avril could no longer stand the howling.

'Oh, Raymond, please shut up!' she snapped.

'I'm *frightened* . . .' Dr Wetherby clutched his briefcase like a teddy bear. 'And I'm never going to get on the Board of Governors now! Not if I'm associated with Blut! I gave his spy the job, for heaven's sake! I was the one who employed Dr Sedukta.'

'Raymond, this is no time to be thinking of your career! If we don't get out of here, we're toast.'

Dr Wetherby began to bawl like a baby.

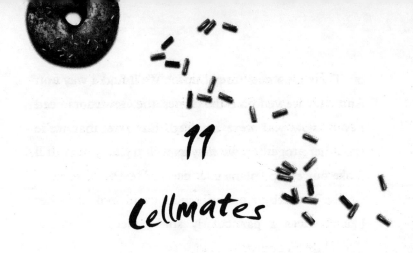

Avril was finding him thoroughly aggravating. It was his fault the clones had run away and his fault she had been kidnapped by Gideon. But she would need his help to escape, so she kept her temper. 'Oh, come on. There's no need to get upset. We'll find a way out. And once we've found the clones, the Governors need never know you were involved. But now that we're stuck here together, we may as well try to get on. It'll make our escape plans a lot easier. Deal?'

Dr Wetherby stopped sobbing and looked at her like she was a particularly stinky piece of cheese. 'Deal,' he hiccuped.

'Right. We're both highly qualified scientists . . . problem-solvers . . . How hard can a little escape plan be?' She cast a determined eye over the room. 'There must be *some* way out.'

Several hours later, Avril was forced to concede that there was not. There were no windows, no hidden passageways and no catflaps. (Avril thought fondly of Auntie Primula, who made sure every room in her house had several catflaps.)

'OK,' she said through gritted teeth. 'Let's recap. We've got the Pretend-to-be-Taken-Ill-Then-Wait-for-Someone-to-Open-the-Door-and-Then-Improvise option. We've got the Shout-Fire-Then-Wait-Until-Someone-Opens-the-Door-and-Then-Improvise option. And finally there's the Loudly-Threaten-Legal-Action-Then-Wait-Until-Someone-Opens-the-Door-and-Then-Improvise option.'

'I still like that last one.' Dr Wetherby was sulking.

'Raymond, I'm just a little worried about this improvising thing. Is there anything in your briefcase we could use? Something to pick the lock.'

'No!' Dr Wetherby gripped his briefcase. 'There's nothing in here.'

'Not even a paper knife, or . . .'

'Listen, you pug-faced old bat, I know what I'm talking about.'

'Hey!' Avril spoke before she could stop herself. 'Don't call me names, Raymond!' She pointed a finger at him. 'I won't put up with it!'

Dr Wetherby pushed her finger away. 'Oh, don't be so silly!'

'It's not silly! It's . . . it's . . .' Avril realised she was shaking, and she was amazed at her reaction to Dr Wetherby's customary taunts. 'I . . . er . . . just don't do it again,' she squeaked, her confidence vanishing as fast as it had appeared. 'That's all.'

Dr Wetherby ignored her. '*I* think that loudly threatening legal action is our best chance. Unless you have any other suggestions? A few silent prayers, perhaps? A little light incantation?' He gestured at the still-heaving tea tray. 'Eat our way through that lot and then *vomit* our way out?'

Avril had completely forgotten about the tea tray.

'Sticky buns!'

'Dear God!' This was the last straw for Dr Wetherby. '*Sticky buns?* This is life and death, woman! Can you think of nothing but baked goods?'

Avril grabbed the largest, stickiest bun from the plate and tore off a hunk. She rolled it up into a squidgy ball and passed it back and forth between her palms. She was thinking hard.

'It might just work . . .' she muttered. She marched up to Dr Wetherby and thrust the gooey mess at him. 'See how sticky this is?'

Dr Wetherby looked at it in disgust.

Avril popped the remainder of the bun in her mouth. 'Here's my plan. I saw this in a film once. They used chewing gum, but I think this will do. We get that big bruiser to come back in here. You have to distract him while I stick this piece of bun in the lock. It will be sticky enough to stop the door from locking properly when he leaves, but soft enough that they won't notice. Hopefully.'

'Hopefully?' Dr Wetherby sneered. 'How scientific of you. All right then. We'll give it a try. Pathetic though it is.'

Avril moved to the door. 'Let's get him in here.'

'By loudly threatening legal action?' Dr Wetherby was suddenly eager.

'If you must.'

It had to work, Avril thought. And it had to work fast.

'. . . And my lawyers are not men to be trifled with! They won a million pounds in damages for the woman who was terminally traumatised by the over-trimming of her pampered pet poodle! They'll have your guts for garters and your spleens for scatter cushions!'

Panting and purple-faced, Dr Wetherby turned to Avril, who was still positioned beside the door.

'Oh, this is hopeless! I've been loudly threatening legal action for nearly an hour. I don't even *have* a lawyer, for heaven's sake!'

'Keep going just a bit longer. I'm sure it's starting to get to him.' It was certainly starting to get to *her*.

Dr Wetherby grimaced and took a deep breath.

'They take their wives to court if their porridge isn't hot enough in the morn –'

The door opened. The cauliflower-eared guard entered.

'So,' Dr Wetherby boomed. 'Finally took our threats seriously, did you?'

The guard looked bemused.

'Threats? The door's soundproofed.'

'Anyway, you're here now,' Avril said, noticing that Dr Wetherby was about to explode. 'And I think Dr Wetherby has something he wants to say. Raymond?'

'Can't be bothered now.'

'Oh, come on. I'm sure there was something . . .'

'No.'

'Just taking the tray.' The security guard picked up the nearly empty tea tray.

'Oh, how kind!' Avril said. 'Perhaps you would like to *comment* on the standard of refreshments, Raymond?'

'Don't care.'

Avril summoned up her most deathly stare and directed it right between Dr Wetherby's eyes.

'*What?*' he snapped at her. 'Are you constipated or something?' Then he sighed. 'Oh, all right then . . .' He turned to their visitor. 'This is appalling. It's been hours since tea! Where's our dinner . . .?'

Avril rolled the ball of cake between her fingers and reached out for the door handle. As quietly as possible, she opened the door an inch and felt for the lock.

‘. . . There will be repercussions, I can assure you . . .’

She pressed the sticky ball into the lock, hardly daring to breathe. It stayed put.

‘Not my problem, pal.’ The guard grinned. ‘Your troubles will be over, anyway, soon as we take you to Room 237 . . .’

For the second time that day, Dr Wetherby burst into noisy tears. This enabled Avril to shut the door again without being heard.

‘Thank you *so* much for visiting!’ She strode cheerfully towards the guard and surreptitiously pilfered the last remaining sandwich. ‘Well, you’d better be going back to your work. We’ll be quite all right without you.’

Sniggering at Dr Wetherby’s sobs, the guard turned to leave. He pulled the heavy door shut.

‘Good one, Raymond!’ Avril clapped him heftily on the back. ‘That loud sobbing was perfect!’

‘I don’t want to die!’ he wailed.

‘Oh, you’re *really* crying.’ Avril sighed. ‘Pull yourself together, Raymond.’

She went to the door and tried the handle. At first it didn’t budge. She pulled it a little harder. With a gentle creak, it opened.

Dr Wetherby rubbed his eyes. 'It actually *worked*?'

'Yes, of course. Now, let's get out of here. We have to find those clones before Dr Sedukta does.'

12

The Play's the Thing

Back in Wretchford Town Library, Lionel rubbed his eyes, blew on his chilly hands, and stared at the computer screen.

The clones were not going to be anywhere near as delighted as he had first thought. In fact, if he told them all he had discovered about the man who had created them, they were going to be appalled.

The articles told of malformed human embryos discovered in glass jars, of strange cloned hands and feet locked away in dark corners of Leviticus. One particularly vivid piece, from a magazine called *Stranger Than Fiction*, to which Lionel now fully intended to start subscribing, wrote about *the blood-curdling screams that filled Leviticus late at night,* and about *the air of evil that hung about Blut's shoulders like a vampire's cloak.* One thing the articles all agreed upon was that Professor Blut had never been seen again. Some speculated that he was in hiding, some that he must be dead, while *Stranger Than Fiction* was adamant that he had been kidnapped by aliens. None of this was going to help the poor clones.

Lionel turned to the last unused page in his notebook and entered the final website that had been listed. It was a lengthy piece on Gideon Blut's disappearance by some investigative journalist, and contained too many tedious facts and figures for Lionel's liking. He scanned through the pages as quickly as he could.

Then he saw something that made him stop.

It was a photograph of a very glamorous and very familiar-looking dark-haired woman, wearing a pair of sunglasses. The caption underneath the picture read: *Serafina Sedukta, international master spy, and one of the most wanted criminals in the world – what does* she *know about Blut's whereabouts? . . . The FBI, who nearly caught up with Sedukta last year, say their recordings of her phone calls reveal that she is in contact with a man calling himself Gideon Blut.*

She was the one who had rung his doorbell late last night!

Lionel was scribbling in his notebook when a

heavy hand on his shoulder made him jump out of his chair.

'*You* again,' said the senior librarian. 'How long have you been in here? Didn't I ban you only last month?'

Lionel was confused. She never came into work until at least nine a.m. Over her hefty shoulder, he could just see the clock on the wall: quarter to seven.

It was quarter to seven in the *evening*.

Lionel squirmed out of the librarian's grip, dived for the door and hurried out of the building. Thankfully his car had not been towed away, though there was a pink slip folded underneath the windscreen wipers. It was not a parking ticket, but what he read made Lionel's knees buckle slightly.

St Swithin's Primary School presents Philomena Dougall's brilliant and original theatrical work, THE CAT and Dick Whittington. *Starring AUGUSTUS THE DOG as 'THE CAT'.*

There was a nicely drawn picture of Augustus filling the bottom half.

Lionel started the spluttering engine and executed a wild three-point turn before roaring back down the high street.

Dr Sedukta had searched everywhere. Abandoned

houses, deserted alleyways, anywhere three frightened clones might be hiding. She had even begun to question passers-by, disregarding secrecy. She could not tell the boss the clones were lost. Of all the people she had worked for – drug dealers, criminal masterminds, crooked politicians – Gideon Blut was the only one she was afraid of. She was in no doubt about what happened to those who incurred his displeasure. He made a point of taking all his new staff to see Room 237, where he gave a well-rehearsed little speech that was now ringing in Dr Sedukta's ears.

'Only two sorts of people are allowed to see this room. Those I can trust, and those who are sent here. I do hope you remain in the first category . . .'

Dr Sedukta was desperate. She had overheard a supermarket checkout girl telling some customers about the extremely tall, red-uniformed man who had pilfered eighteen pounds seventy-one pence worth of goods from the store that very morning. The clones were definitely in Wretchford, she just didn't know *where*. Now it was getting dark again. Despite the freezing weather and her customary coolness, she was sweating. She was going to have to tell Gideon.

She stopped outside the library and fumbled in her pocket for her mobile phone with shaking hands.

Suddenly a giant poster on the library door caught her eye. The picture was what first held her attention, but the large writing made her move closer.

AUGUSTUS THE DOG as 'THE CAT' . . .

Dr Sedukta dropped the phone back into her pocket. 'Excuse me,' she purred at a passing policeman. 'Could you tell me the quickest way to St Swithin's school . . .?'

As the audience gathered in the school hall, Eddy tried to remain calm. There was no sign of Lionel, and it looked as if they were going to have to go ahead with the play.

'Five minutes!' Wilfred told Eddy, pushing the cardboard chariot into the wings. It was newly painted with three slapdash coats of gilt, and decorated with a smattering of plastic rubies. 'You'd better give Augustus his call.'

Eddy moved along to Augustus's dressing room. The rest of the cast had been herded into the toilets, leaving the dressing room solely for his use, and Bonaparte had pasted a cardboard star to the door. Eddy glared at it and went in without bothering to knock.

Augustus was stretched out on his chaise longue,

tucking into a takeaway pizza. There was a half-eaten bunch of grapes on the floor, and an enormous vase of fresh flowers on the windowsill. He was wearing a silk eye-mask.

'Old Boot-Face Dougall seemed to think I might like a pizza,' he said, as Eddy pulled up a corner of the mask. 'Give me strength for the show.'

'Augustus! You didn't *speak* to her?'

'Course not.' He chewed at a slice of pizza. 'We great actors need no *words* to communicate, you know.'

'Look.' Eddy struggled to control her temper. 'You'd better behave yourself, Augustus. Just stay quiet, ride around in your chariot and get it over with so we can get out of here. *No funny business.* Got it?' She stamped out and slammed the door shut just as a tuneless piano chord from Miss Dougall out front announced the opening song of the show.

'It's under control,' Dr Sedukta was telling her mobile phone as she slid along St Swithin's Street and through the school gates. 'I've tracked them down to a school. St Swithin's.'

'*A school? They are* out in public*? This is most unsatisfactory.*'

'I'm on to it, professor.' Dr Sedukta's smooth hair

was starting to frizz very slightly. She chewed a dark red talon. 'I'll bring them to you.'

'*No, thank you. You have taken up quite enough of my time and patience already.*'

Dr Sedukta almost whimpered.

'*I will send Dr Crump's clone. It will be able to take them away without raising their suspicions. You just keep an eye on them until it gets there. And for heaven's sake, do not draw attention to yourself or the Non-Viables* in any way.'

Augustus's face stared down at Dr Sedukta from a sign saying, '*See Augustus the Dog onstage for the first time!!!*'

'B-but if something *should* happen?' Dr Sedukta tried make her trembling voice sound casual. 'If the dog should speak . . .?'

'*I hope you do not allow it to come to that, Serafina. But if it does, you know what to do.*'

Dr Sedukta stared down at the silver ring on the fourth finger of her right hand. With her thumb, she twisted it gently. 'In an emergency . . .'

'*In an emergency . . .*'

13

My Name Is Mr Dog

Lionel was out of breath when he arrived at St Swithin's school hall. He tried in vain to dredge up a morsel of oxygen, but the shock of seeing Bonaparte onstage was too much for him.

'Oo-ar,' the clone was bellowing happily. 'Oo-ar.'

Where was Eddy? Lionel squinted through the darkness and scanned the rows of chairs, but there were no familiar faces.

Except for one. The dark-haired woman in sunglasses slipping into a spare seat in the front row, staring intently up at the stage, her eyes fixed on Bonaparte.

Lionel's racing heart almost stopped dead. And then –

A dreadful creaking announced the arrival of a tatty-looking chariot. Augustus glared out at the audience behind the bright lights. They had no appreciation of the finer points of his art. Philistines. Then he noticed something. Amongst the blue rinses and shabby hand-me-downs, in the front row, sat a woman of true class. She *dripped* with distinction. Nobody wore sunglasses indoors unless they were truly important. She must be a West End producer, come to discover him!

Augustus hopped out of the chariot and pranced forwards, ready to dazzle the talent scout with his brilliance.

Dr Sedukta was on full alert. What was the wretched mutt about to do? Eyes bright, ears pricked and paws aloft, he was taking a deep theatrical breath. Sedukta remembered Gideon's instructions. She must silence the dog . . .

Several things happened at once. Lionel saw a tiny dart fly from Sedukta's ring. 'Watch out!' he shouted . . .

Augustus felt something whiz past his right ear . . .

And Bonaparte sprang to the front of the stage, pulling off his hat and waving a sheaf of grubby papers. 'Ladies and gentlemen!' His voice was trembling with anticipation. 'Allow me to present my contribution to this remarkable piece of theatre!'

There was a bemused silence. The audience stared

up at the extraordinary figure on the stage as he warbled a little to find his starting note.

In a fury Dr Sedukta twisted off her silver tranquilliser ring. 'Blast!' she spat as it rolled out of her hand and under her chair. The little girl seated behind her picked it up. 'Hands off! It's mine!'

The girl poked her tongue out and handed the ring to her friend. 'Pass it on,' she giggled.

'This song,' said Bonaparte, 'is entitled "My Name Is Mr Dog".'

Dr Sedukta leapt from her seat and began to clamber over the rows of chairs, eyes fixed on the ring as it passed from hand to sweaty hand. 'Give that back!' she screeched, above Bonaparte's singing.

From the other side of the hall, Lionel saw exactly what was happening and began climbing over chairs himself, desperate to reach the ring before Dr Sedukta did.

'For yea, my name is Mr Dog!
Hooray, my name is Mr Dog!
All say, my name is Mr Dog!
My name is Mr Dog.'

* * *

Breathless with excitement, Bonaparte finished his first chorus. Shading his eyes with a shaking hand, he peered into the auditorium.

'Dost please thee?' he called.

Miss Dougall gurgled slightly.

'Then I shall continue!' Bonaparte tapped his foot on the floor to re-establish his rhythm, and took up the second verse.

Backstage, Eddy was frozen in shock.

Wilfred tugged her sleeve. 'Eddy. Your uncle . . . It's the worst song I've ever heard.'

Eddy dared to peep around the wings, where her eye was drawn to a disturbance out in the auditorium. To her astonishment, she could see Lionel leaping unathletically across the lap of a bewildered grandmother six rows back. *Lionel! I knew you'd come.* She turned to Wilfred. 'You're absolutely right. We've got to stop him.' She spotted the turnip basket. 'Pass me one of those turnips.'

Beginning the third verse, Bonaparte was striking a pose. He lowered his quavering voice to a dramatic whisper, oblivious to the commotion out front.

Eddy took aim with the turnip but her throw went wide and it rolled out into the audience.

Dr Sedukta pounced on a freckled boy beside the

middle aisle just as the ring reached his hands. Lionel dived wildly across two rows and managed to grasp the boy by the trouser leg.

'Give it here, brat!' Dr Sedukta twisted his ears.

'No! Don't let her have it!' Lionel gasped. 'Please . . .'

Alarmed, the boy let go of the ring. It tumbled to the floor and spun down the aisle, with Lionel and Dr Sedukta in hot pursuit.

Bonaparte's performance finished with a flourish. He bounded over to Augustus. 'Dost thou wish to hear any part again?'

'Good grief,' said Augustus.

Luckily the audience was too distracted by the fight that had broken out in its midst to realise that it was the dog who had just spoken. Lionel and Dr Sedukta both had a hold on the ring.

'Let go!' Dr Sedukta was sweating as she struggled with the old man, trying to break his grip with wild karate chops.

'Never!' Lionel almost pulled away from her, but she administered a nasty blow to his funny bone. '*Owww!*'

The ring flew up into the air. Lionel and Dr Sedukta elbowed and shoved at each other, reaching out to be the first to grab it as it spun back down towards the ground . . .

It was Lionel who got the first touch. Fumbling blindly with his fingertips to secure his catch, his thumb brushed against the firing mechanism etched into the silver. A tiny tranquilliser dart shot out of the ring, and met Dr Sedukta's right earlobe.

She was unconscious even before she hit the floor, approximately one and a half seconds later.

'Shall I provide an encore?' Bonaparte was still flushed with success.

'*NO!*' Miss Dougall sprang to her feet from the heap she had fallen into somewhere in the middle of the second verse. 'Not again . . .'

Bonaparte's face plummeted like a doomed elevator. 'Didst it displease thee?' He lowered his sheets of paper and hung his head. 'I am exceeding sorry.'

'INTERVAL!' Miss Dougall cried, as Bonaparte drooped his way out into the wings.

A battered Lionel hauled himself up on to the stage as the audience began to head for the exit. He spotted the first dart where it had landed on the floor and put it carefully inside his handkerchief. Then he scooped Augustus up and went into the wings.

'You've been followed,' he said, ushering Eddy towards a side door against which a sniffling Bonaparte was leaning. 'There's a woman in the audience – she tried to shoot you –'

'Oh, rubbish,' Augustus snapped. 'That woman was a top theatrical producer, not some common criminal.'

'– with this.' Lionel held out the dart.

'Well,' Augustus said. 'I'm sure she's a top theatrical producer in her spare time.'

'We've got to get out of here.' Lionel opened the side door.

'Eddy! W-wait!' Wilfred was gazing at the four of them, astonished that a dog had just appeared to speak. 'W-what on earth is going on?'

'Wilfred, I can't explain,' Eddy said. 'I . . . I have to go . . .'

'You can't!'

'Eddy, come on,' said Lionel, giving a glance over his shoulder to check that Dr Sedukta was still unconscious.

Eddy brushed off Lionel's hand and stared back at Wilfred. 'I don't *want* to go,' she said. 'I just want to be normal.' She did not know whether she was talking to Wilfred, Lionel or herself, but it was Lionel who responded.

'But you're not normal,' he said softly. 'You can't stay here. It's too dangerous.'

Eddy looked at the others. Bonaparte was blowing his nose on his sleeve and clutching his song sheets. Augustus was trying to get comfortable in Lionel's arms.

'I'm sorry.' With tears in her eyes, Eddy turned back to Wilfred. 'I have to go with my family.'

'*What*'s d-dangerous? Eddy, tell me what's going on! You're my friend . . .'

Wilfred's voice rang after them as Lionel hurried the three clones through the door, almost drowning out Bonaparte's sobbing.

'I did but wish to honour Mr Dog with a musical tribute! Did I do *very* wrong?'

Eddy was glad of the distraction. She was trying very hard not to cry herself. 'Well, it was rather silly, Bony.'

'He did but wish to honour me with a musical tribute.' Augustus glared at her. 'Can you blame him?'

'And I did also wish Mr Shakespeare to be proud of me.'

'Oh, Bony,' Eddy said. 'That's very sweet. Although I have a sneaking suspicion that things got so mixed up in the explosion that you're more likely to have Shakespeare's bravery and Napoleon's writing skills . . . I know you only wanted to please everyone . . .'

'*And* honour me with a musical tribute . . .'

'. . . but it might have put us in even more danger.

You told everyone the story of how we were created!'

'Oh, please,' said Augustus. 'As if anyone could make head or tail of that drivel.'

Bonaparte let out a howl.

'There's no time for recriminations now.' Lionel said. 'Let's hurry. There could be more of them.'

At the far end of the corridor, a door opened.

'Don't move!' Lionel hissed. 'We don't know who it is.'

Eddy reached for Bonaparte's hand and looked at Augustus, still in Lionel's arms.

'Get ready to run,' she whispered.

'Who are you?' Lionel called. 'Identify yourself!'

The figure stopped. It reached out for a light switch.

'There's no need for that,' it said cheerfully.

A light flicked on.

'I'm here now, children! I've found you! Everything's going to be all right.'

The three clones stared. They spoke with one breath.

'Avril!'

14

The Missing Clone

Clutching respectively a leather briefcase and a ham sandwich, Dr Wetherby and Avril began to tiptoe down the narrow corridor outside the library. They passed door after door marked with neat black lettering. *Experiment Room 1 . . . Experiment Room 2 . . .*

Reaching a small, closed door at the end of the corridor, Dr Wetherby searched for something to batter it with. Discounting Avril, whose head might be too soft, he seized a nearby chair and swung it repeatedly at the door.

'This should do it!' he said as Avril and her ham sandwich wheezed up behind him.

'Have you . . . tried the . . . handle?'

'Honestly, woman, as if they're going to lock us in that room like sardines and then leave another door wide open.' He tried the handle. 'See?'

It opened. He almost blushed.

'Come on then, you old boot.'

But Avril did not move. She was staring at a sign on the door.

Medical Centre.

'Raymond, don't go in there!'

It was too late. Dr Wetherby was continuing to tiptoe. He tiptoed right through the doorway and into the room.

'Raymond!'

Avril abandoned all pretence at tiptoeing. She lunged into the room to drag him back.

A cluster of white-coated figures, their backs towards the door, was gathered around an operating table in the middle of the large room. Gideon Blut's golden head was at the centre of the group. He was holding a metal tape measure. As one member of the small gathering shifted slightly, Avril realised that someone was sitting on the operating table.

It might have been a small child, or a frail, shrunken adult, but whatever it was, its body was deformed, its limbs misshapen and its muscles wasted. Three gigantic eyes floated in outsized sockets at the top of its head, and the lower part of its face was missing.

Avril could not move. She gazed at this creature in horror, pity and revulsion. For a dazed moment, she found a distant memory popping into her head – her first Biology lesson at senior school, when a dead lab rat was brought out for the teacher to dissect. The honour of making the first incision was offered to Avril. She had been appalled at the very thought. The worst thing was that the rat was still warm, its small, beady eyes wide open.

Now, in the dreadful present, Avril stared at this half-human: the otherworldly lab rat of Gideon's Mission. It was worse even than she had been imagining. How could a scientist do something like this?

'What on *earth* . . .?' Dr Wetherby whispered.

Gideon leaned forwards with his tape measure and stretched it down the captive's twisted spine. 'Eighty-seven centimetres,' he said. The group scribbled on clipboards. 'Consistent with our findings. I think we have extracted enough information from this particular specimen. Take it to Room 237 for immediate destruction, please.'

Another thuggish security guard stepped up to the operating table as Gideon busied himself with his own clipboard, his brow dimpled with concentration. The clone on the table was shrinking back from the thug, drawing up its twisted legs in a hopeless attempt to resist. Suddenly, Gideon put a hand up in front of the guard. 'Wait a moment,' he said. He reached over to a tray and picked up a small instrument. 'There is just one more thing about this Non-Viable that I would like to observe. Pass me that bowl, if you please.'

The malformed clone's three eyes suddenly alighted on Avril and Dr Wetherby. If it had had a mouth, it might have called out to them; instead, it simply stretched out an imploring, withered arm.

Desperate as she was to help this poor soul, Avril knew that Gideon might follow its gaze and turn around. She seized Dr Wetherby by the briefcase and hauled him backwards through the open doorway. Their eyes met.

'Run!'

They set off back down the long corridor. Despite his shaking legs, Dr Wetherby raced ahead, past the library, where the corridor bent around to the left. He found a row of doors on one side of the corridor, and began trying the handles of each one.

'No use,' he panted, as Avril wheezed round the corner. 'They're all locked.' He moved to a wide set of double doors at the end of the row and rattled them. 'This is hopeless! It's like a fortress in here. A fortress full of damn lunatics!' He gave the doors an angry kick. 'Let's keep going.'

They were just about to start running again when the double doors swung slowly open.

Behind the doors were five glass cases, each one about two metres high and a metre wide. They were filled with a transparent, bluish solution that bubbled occasionally. And in four of the five cases was a copy of Avril.

For a moment, Avril herself was as frozen in time as they were. She stared at the copies, unable to move. It was like looking in a distorted mirror. They were not perfect copies. One had an outsized head and too much hair; another appeared to have an extra hand. Each of them had cold, empty eyes. The words SOILED were stamped in large letters on the outside of these four cases. The fifth case bore the words AVRIL CRUMP II – READY FOR USE.

It was empty.

Avril doubled over, trying not to be sick. She waited for a vicious comment from Dr Wetherby. But he just gazed at the four ruined Avrils.

'He can't do this! It's illegal! It's wr –'

At that moment, triggered by the cupboard doors swinging further open, an alarm began to ring.

There were shouts from the Medical Centre down the corridor, followed by rapid footsteps.

'Quick!' Knowing she had to recover herself, Avril spotted a neon sign above a small alcove. *Fire Escape*. She dragged a shocked Dr Wetherby towards the alcove.

'Stay still,' she whispered, 'until they go past us.'

Like the gum-in-the-door trick, Avril had seen this in the movies. The trouble was that, even in the movies, the trick never worked.

With much shouting and thudding, a group of heavy-set figures raced straight past them, the cauliflower-eared thug at their head. They did not turn back.

'Good Lord . . .' Avril could hardly believe it.

'Come on.' Dr Wetherby opened the window on to the fire escape. Avril followed him out, the icy wind surprising her and taking her breath away. They took the wrought-iron steps three at a time, reached the bottom and looked around. It was growing dark, and low-burning lamps on the walls of the manor cast only a faint light. The outlines of thick trees were black against the dark blue sky. It took a moment for Avril's eyes to adjust. They had clearly come down at the side of the house, as a gravelled forecourt was just visible around the corner. There was a long driveway stretching off it.

'That way!' Avril pointed.

They began to run again, not looking back. The air was freezing, and very still. The only sounds were their tired feet pounding the gravel, the faint alarm up at the manor and Avril's wheezing breathing.

'We'll have to get past that gate!' Dr Wetherby called. A tall iron gate with wide-set bars was indeed looming as they neared the end of the long driveway. '*I'll* be able to squeeze through the bars,' he added over his shoulder. '*You'll* have to go over the top.'

Avril nodded miserably, recalling her spectacular failures at school sports day high-jump contests. For a moment, she could even hear the chants of '*Avril Crump's a bald, fat lump, Avril Crump can't even jump*' all over again.

'Get a move on!' Dr Wetherby had thrown his briefcase through and was squeezing himself between two bars. With a pained grunt or two, he just managed to slip through to the other side and set off at a run. Avril flexed her hands and began to haul herself upwards. She was less than half a metre up before she knew she was stuck.

'Raymond, help me!'

'What are you still doing up there?' But Dr Wetherby was already running back. He reached through the gate and began to shove at her bottom. 'Come on, woman!' he gasped. 'We must hurry!'

Loud shouts could suddenly be heard from the house. This and Dr Wetherby's shoving were all Avril needed. She grasped her way up the iron bars and swung over the top. In her triumph, she let go.

'Ouch.'

The shouts were getting louder. Bright torches appeared. It would only be a matter of time.

'We need to get further away.' Avril staggered to her feet and glanced around. Away from the lights of the manor it was even darker, and the thin moonlight was blocked by trees. She could just make out a narrow pathway leading downhill. 'They brought us here in a car, so this must go to a main road.'

'How can you be sure?'

'Well, it's the only route that'll take us away from the manor,' said Avril, setting off as fast as she could, 'so unless you want to retrace our steps . . .'

She had only to wait a moment. Dr Wetherby pushed past her and hurried on ahead along the wooded pathway.

'So, Dr Crump, *if* we ever get to a main road, what is your plan?'

'Well, we haven't a moment to lose, Raymond! We

have to find the clones before Gideon gets to them.' Gideon's velvety voice was ringing in Avril's head: '*Take it to Room 237 for immediate destruction*' . . . She swallowed. 'The last place we saw them was at Leviticus, so I suppose we should go back there . . .'

Dr Wetherby stopped, causing Avril to waddle straight into him in the darkness. 'Brilliant idea,' he said, when he had got back on his feet and checked for permanent damage. 'Of course, you do know *exactly* how to get to Leviticus from the middle of nowhere? Are we just going to hop on a bus? Or do you fancy trying to read the stars? Or maybe you could just whip up one of your stupid mop mixtures and explode us out of here, fatso!'

Deep down inside Avril, something snapped. Before she even knew what she was doing, she had rushed at Dr Wetherby with a desperate head-butt. 'DON'T CALL ME FATSO!'

Dr Wetherby toppled to the frozen ground again as Avril barged into him.

'I've had enough of your name-calling for one day!' Standing over him, Avril clenched her fists. 'In fact, I've had enough of name-calling *for ever*. You're not my boss any more, Raymond. I'm resigning!'

Dr Wetherby looked up at her in amazement.

'I'm trying to rescue the only friends I ever had, and all you've done is bully and belittle me. I may be fat and bald, Raymond, but I'm not a bad person. At least I care about the clones! What do *you* care about? Your rules, your stupid Codes of Conduct . . .'

'Now hold on just one moment!' Dr Wetherby scrambled to his feet and backed away from her, smoothing his hair and straightening his tie. 'Believe it or not, *I care about science.* I care about madmen like Blut perverting it for their own ends. Science is about precision, about accuracy. *It is not about power and it is not about glory.*' He slammed his fist into the palm of his hand. He was sweating. 'I treat science with respect, Dr Crump, because otherwise –' he jerked a thumb back in the direction of Gargoyle Manor – '*that* is what happens.'

'Raymond . . .'

'I *do* care about finding these clones . . .'

'Oh, Raymond, thank you . . .'

'. . . but they must be dealt with by the proper authorities.'

'Destroyed, you mean!'

Dr Wetherby looked older for a moment. His face sank into deep, weary lines. 'I don't know. I don't want to destroy anyone. I just like to play by the rules. That's all.'

There was a silence.

'I'm sorry, Raymond. There's nothing wrong with rules.' She gave him a hesitant grin. 'I just prefer them when they're broken . . .' Dr Wetherby's frown-lines remained. Avril wanted to touch him on the arm, but her hand stopped in mid-air. He did not look as though he wanted to be touched. 'I'm sorry I mistook you.'

'And I am . . . I am –' he pursed his lips, as if he did not want to let the words out – 'I *regret* my irritability. You are . . . a good scientist, Dr Crump. And you are brave.'

Avril had never felt more like crying.

'Now,' Dr Wetherby said, smoothing his already-smooth hair and adjusting his labcoat again. 'Shouldn't we be hurrying?' He turned around and set off down the pathway.

Blinking back tears, Avril followed. She was thinking so hard about Dr Wetherby's outburst that she hardly noticed the path beginning to get wider or the frozen, muddy ground becoming concrete beneath her feet.

'I think we're on this *main road* of yours,' Dr Wetherby called to her. He was beginning to sound irritable again, which jolted Avril back into reality. She stopped thinking and took a good look around. Over the top of Dr Wetherby's bobbing head, she suddenly spotted something. She squinted a little, but her eyesight was good. She was not imagining it.

'There's a signpost! Quickly! What does it say?'

Dr Wetherby hurried towards the thin signpost. It was nothing more than a splintered plank nailed to a tree. He wrinkled his nose and scrubbed at it gingerly with a sleeve before leaning closer to read it.

'Wretchford-on-the-Reeke, five miles.'

'Wretchford!' Avril was delighted, not a common reaction to mention of the town. 'I told the clones that's where I live! We can start there, and if we can't find them, we can still pick up my car. That'll make looking for them a lot easier.'

Without waiting for his reply, she was off. Five miles. They had to hurry.

15

Home Sweet Home

'Lady Avril! 'Tis truly thee!'

Bonaparte hurtled down the corridor and flung himself upon the short, fat, bald, white-coated figure.

'So much has occurred since last we saw thee! What excitement, what adventure, what *stew*!'

'Good to see you too, Bonaparte. Good to see all of you.'

'*Avril?*' Eddy took one step forward. 'Is it *really* you?'

'Of course it's me,' she beamed. 'Who else would it be? My evil twin or something?' She guffawed with laughter.

'But . . .' Eddy was confused. Now that Avril was actually here in front of them, it did not feel the way she had imagined that it would. She did not know why she was not running and hugging her like Bony was. 'How did you know we were here?' was all she could say.

'Maternal instinct,' came the smooth reply. 'Now, are we all ready to go? I'm taking you to my holiday cottage in the woods. We're going to live there now. It's much nicer than Wretchford.' She reached down and picked Augustus up.

Standing some distance away, Lionel coughed.

'Lionel, of course!' Eddy pulled him forward and held on to his hand, not wanting to let go. 'You must meet Lionel. He's been wonderful to us, Avril. He's saved our lives and everything!'

'Enchanted,' Lionel began, extending his free hand. But she merely turned away.

'We really must hurry.' She gave Bonaparte a shove in the direction of the doors. 'It's very late. My car is just outside. Come along, Eddy!'

'You'd better go,' said Lionel, removing his hand from Eddy's grip.

'I suppose so . . .'

'I'll be fine.' Lionel gave her a gentle push. 'You're with Avril now.'

'EDDY!' came the shout from down the corridor.

'You called me Edna before,' Eddy said, as she caught up with the others. She looked up at the oddly unfamiliar round, pink face, which did not look down at her. 'After your train set . . .'

'Great! A ride in the sports car!' Augustus remembered what Avril had said about her car. He wriggled happily in her arms as Bonaparte reached over to tie his long ears up into a convertible-ready knot on top of his head. 'I'm so glad you found us, dear Avril,' he said. 'This is *much* more like it.'

'But what about Lionel?' Eddy tried to turn around as they were marched onwards. Lionel was staring after them, bewildered.

'Oh, don't worry about him. You can invite him over. He really *must* come and visit.'

'Goodbye!' Lionel called.

'Lionel, we'll phone you . . .' Eddy just had time to glimpse his sad, tired face before the door shut behind them.

The winter darkness enveloped them as they emerged into the playground. There were only three cars in the small parking area: Lionel's yellow Mini, a rusty blue Ford, and a sparkling clean small white van.

'Where's yours?' Augustus glanced about.

They were led towards the white van. The back door opened with the touch of a button. 'Get in.'

'But you said your car was a little green convertible . . .' Eddy spoke up even before Augustus's jaw dropped.

'I only use that for special occasions. Besides, there wouldn't be room for all three of you. It's really very comfortable in here. Lots of room to spread out.' She beamed again. 'Oh, come on! It'll be fun. And it's only a short ride to the cottage. There'll be toasted teacakes waiting when we get there!'

'We'd better get in, Bony.' Eddy grasped his hand and began to help him into the back of the van.

Bonaparte was curious to discover if teacakes were as good as stew. They hauled Augustus, who was still too shocked to speak, up into the van beside them just as the door was slammed. A moment later, an engine started up.

Bonaparte settled down on one of the benches that ran along the side of the van and scrunched his legs up to make room for the others.

Eddy was not feeling very happy, but she tried to smile. At least Bonaparte seemed to have recovered from the embarrassment of his peculiar performance.

Augustus was muttering to himself. 'I was promised a sports car . . .'

'Come on, Gus . . . Augustus.' Eddy forced

another of her smiles. 'We have nothing to be afraid of.' As soon as the words were out of her mouth, she wondered why she had said them. After all, the other two did not seem at all frightened. Bonaparte was excited about the teacakes, Augustus merely indignant at the mode of transport. She was the only one who was afraid.

In the front seat, Avril II jammed her foot on the accelerator and sped away.

Half an hour later, the white van drew to a sharp halt. The clones felt it reverse, then stop again. The back door was suddenly thrown open and an icy breeze whipped into the van. It was almost too dark now to see.

'Out you get.'

Eddy stumbled out first, followed by Bonaparte. She looked about, her eyes watering with the cold. There was just enough winter moonlight filtering through the overhanging trees to allow them to see their surroundings. They were in a large clearing in a thick wood. The van had been parked outside a low, white building with a flat roof. It had no windows and a steel door.

'Is this your holiday home?' Eddy tried to persuade her lips to smile. 'It's . . . lovely . . .'

'That's *it*?' The voice came from inside the van, where Augustus was folding his paws across his chest. He stared at the building. '*This* is where I'm supposed to live? This *bunker*? Forget it.' He glared at them, blaming all three in equal measure. 'Take me to a hotel! I am a distinguished actor! This place is not fit for a dog.'

'Augustus!' Eddy said nervously. 'Don't be rude.'

Augustus swore at her and turned his back.

'Be not disheartened, Mr Dog . . .' Bonaparte peered into the van. ''Tis our new home!'

'I don't know why *you're* so enthusiastic about this dump,' Augustus said. 'Doesn't look like a place with even the most basic stew-making facilities, if you ask me.'

Bonaparte gasped. 'Lady Avril? Is this true?'

'Oh, don't you worry. You'll stew all right.'

Relieved, Bonaparte turned back to the van. 'Mr Dog, I beg thee, come inside. I shall carry thee if thou art too weary to walk.'

Augustus scowled. '*One night*,' he said. 'One night only.'

The thick steel door opened smoothly with a large key, and a very bright light shone out of the open doorway. Eddy closed her eyes, dazzled for a moment, but also because she was suddenly worried about what she would see. She had had such high hopes of arriving home with Avril, and she could hardly bear for them to be dashed. She opened her eyes.

It was a large, white-walled, rather empty room, with three doors leading off it. The floor was tiled, and covered in several places with thin rugs. There was a small blue sofa and an armchair. An open-plan kitchen area displayed a kettle and a sink. A packet of biscuits stood on the clean work surface. Light strains of bland orchestral music filtered out of a speaker in one corner. There was a strong, rather sweet smell in the air.

There was nothing wrong with it. There was also nothing right with it.

'How nice!' Eddy said. She was relieved that it was not as bad as she had been anticipating, although it did feel a little . . . well, *clinical*. It was cold too; no sign of a fire to warm their freezing bones. The thought of Lionel's cosy and cluttered little home popped into her mind, but Eddy quickly squashed this memory. There was no point in thinking of the past. Avril was their future. 'I'm sure we'll be very happy here, Avril.'

A hand was waved at her in reply. 'Yeah, yeah . . .' Avril II had seized the packet of biscuits without offering them around and was already almost halfway through, spraying crumbs over the hungry clones as she walked past. There was no sign of toasted teacakes. 'Sit down. I've got a few things to do.' She opened one of the three doors, which was numbered 237, peered inside it, closed it, wandered to another door, labelled 'Document Storage', peered inside that one and went through. 'Don't come in here, any of you. It's *private*.' She gave them a rather ghastly smile. 'Back in a mo.'

'Well, I was right.' Augustus had taken up residence on the sofa. 'It *is* a complete dump!'

'Come on, Augustus, it's not that bad. It's just a bit chilly. Avril probably hasn't stayed here for a while, that's all.' Eddy moved for the armchair at the same time as Bonaparte. Fortunately he was so thin that there was enough room for both of them. His head was drooping.

''Tis a dreadful sight to see Mr Dog without his creature comforts,' Bonaparte sighed.

'Hey!' Augustus snapped. 'Less of the *creature*.'

'Look, you two.' Eddy rubbed her eyes. The cold was making her sleepy. 'We're just going to have to lump it, I'm afraid. If we care about Avril at all, this is where we will live, and this is where we will be happy. And we do care about Avril, don't we?'

Bonaparte nodded. Augustus ignored the question.

'Indeed I do, Miss Eddy. Although I cannot but think that Lady Avril is not as she was.'

'Yeah.' Augustus looked at Eddy accusingly. 'Me too.'

Eddy refused to agree. Bonaparte had said exactly what she had been thinking since Avril had arrived at the school, but she did not want to admit it to herself. This was not what she had hoped for. She had thought that finding Avril would be the start of an ordinary life. But she did not feel right here, and she was missing Lionel and Wilfred desperately.

'Oh!' she said suddenly, her eyes alighting on a telephone on the wall. 'Look, you two! It's a phone!'

She received no reply. Bonaparte was too dejected and Augustus had decided to ignore her.

'We can call Lionel! I *think* I remember his phone number. It was on that funny sign outside his house.' Eddy ran over to the phone and picked it up to see if it worked. It buzzed gently at her. This was an improvement! She only wished she had Wilfred's phone number too.

'Are you trying to use the phone?' Avril II suddenly demanded, peering around the Document Storage door.

'No, Avril,' Eddy said.

Avril II came out and closed the door behind her, tucking a piece of paper very carefully into her pocket. 'Well, don't,' she said. 'It's a private line, anyway.' She looked closely at all three of them. 'You look pretty dirty. You –' she pointed at Eddy – 'could do with a bit of disinfecting.'

'*Disinfecting?*'

'I mean washing.' Avril II smiled. 'I have a friend I'm going to take you to see. He's very keen to meet you, but he is rather partial to hygiene. You'll need a jolly good shower.' She handed Eddy a towel, a new bar of soap and a large bottle of shampoo. 'Through that door,' she said, pointing at one of the rooms she hadn't been in to.

Eddy hesitated. 'Do the other two get to have a nice hot shower as well?'

'It's not really necessary for them.'

Augustus sniggered at Eddy. '*We're* not the filthy ones.'

'Hurry along now!' Avril II pulled her towards the door. 'We haven't got all night. Just leave your clothes in the basket. There's a new outfit for you in there.'

Eddy put a hand on the door handle, uncertain what to do. She was afraid of leaving Bonaparte and

Augustus. 'Will you two be all right?'

'They'll be fine!' Avril II opened the door and pushed Eddy into the bathroom.

Like the living room, the bathroom was white-walled and almost empty, with the addition of a tiled shower in one corner. Eddy looked back at the door. She was suddenly tempted to run out, seize the other two and escape into the forest. But what would Avril think? Eddy was clinging to the hope that she was simply in a strange mood. She would become the Avril they had first met soon enough, wouldn't she?

Eddy began to undress for her shower.

Outside, Avril II turned to the others, her eyes stone cold. 'Now for you two. In there,' she barked, jerking her thumb towards the third door, labelled 237.

'How dare you adopt that tone with me!' said Augustus. 'That's no way to speak to one of imperial heritage, Crump-face.'

Avril II took a deep breath. When she spoke again, her words were honey-coated. 'Go . . . through . . . that . . . door. *Please.*'

'That's more like it.' Augustus got up. 'I hope for your sake,' he said, 'that *that* room is a sight more comfortable than this one. Come on, Bony. Oh –' he stopped – 'one more thing. I like to be woken with a hot cup of tea at ten o'clock in the morning. A fresh croissant will win you extra points.'

Bonaparte trotted behind Augustus as a smirking Avril II opened the door to Room 237.

'Sleep tight,' she said.

16

ROOM 237

Wretchford's roads were deserted at this time of night, so Avril raced her little green convertible through the streets. It was the route she took to Leviticus every day, out to the north of Wretchford, but she didn't normally travel at this speed.

'Slow down, woman!' Dr Wetherby howled, buckling up his seat belt with shaking hands as they shot past Wretchford Common and hurtled towards the high street. 'I'd like us to get there in one piece, if you don't mind. Well, one piece and one balding lump,' he added, grasping at normality by returning to his old insults.

Avril ignored his wail as she deliberately pressed her foot even harder on the accelerator.

* * *

Room 237 was pitch black. It became blacker still as Avril II shut – and then locked – the door behind them.

'Find a light switch, Bony.' Augustus's voice echoed. 'Sounds big in here. This is more like it. Although that smell is getting worse.'

'I canst not find any such switch, Mr Dog.'

'Oh, come on! There must be one somewhere.'

From outside, Augustus could hear the phone ringing. It rang three times, then stopped.

'What?' Avril II's voice came through the door. 'I'm busy . . . Yes, I was just about to do that.'

'Bony . . .' Augustus did not want to admit that he was afraid of this terrible darkness. 'I'm starting to lose my patience.'

'Forgive me, Mr Dog, I . . .'

Avril's voice dropped to a whisper. 'Bring the girl to you *now*? You want to begin experimenting on her? What's the rush? . . . Well, if they ran away, they're hardly likely to come back on the off-chance that they might be able to rescue her, are they? . . . All right, all right, you're the boss, I'm just the stupid clone.'

Augustus froze. 'Are you listening to this?' he hissed at Bonaparte.

'I can hear nothing, Mr Dog.'

Augustus's ears were pricked up.

'Don't worry, they're locked in Room 237. I haven't let the stuff in yet . . . *Yes*, I'll get the girl out of the shower and drive her over to you now. I'll come back and get rid of the other two later.'

'Mr Dog, I am exceeding sorry, but my search for this light switch of which thou hast spoken is proving fruitless.'

Augustus let out a low whimper.

'Oh, Mr Dog! I beg thee, be not downhearted! I will find this switch . . .' Bonaparte's voice moved further away, 'if it be the last thing that ever I do.'

Augustus was weak at all four knees.

'Bony!' he hissed again. 'Didn't you hear that?'

'Hear what, Mr Dog?' Bony sounded cheerful. 'I do not possess thy remarkable canine hearing.'

'She's going to kill us, Bony! She's going to experiment on Eddy, and then she's going to let some stuff in here that will *get rid* of us!'

'This is regretful news, Mr Dog.'

'*Regretful news?*' Augustus bounded to where Bonaparte's voice was coming from. Outside, he heard the van start up. 'A slight cold is regretful news, Bony. A recently deceased pet is regretful news. Kidnapping and cold-blooded murder –' he could barely speak – 'that's positively *wretched* news! And we're not the ones receiving the news, you Napoleonic nincompoop! We *are* the news!'

'Lady Avril doth plan to *murder* us?'

'Yes! Obviously it's been her plan all along! I *knew* there was something strange about her, but nobody listened to me, did they?'

Bonaparte began to sob.

'All right, Bony, just calm down.'

'I am not afeard, Mr Dog. I am but saddened by our betrayal. I fear nothing because I am in the presence of a great hero, a dog of imperial bearing and a bravery of which I can only dream. I know that thou wilt save us.'

Augustus gulped. 'Me? I was rather hoping *you* might have an idea.'

'Oh, no, Mr Dog. I would not presume to offer my foolish ideas when thou art certain to be bursting with superior ones.'

'Quite, quite . . . but if you *were* to offer an inferior idea . . . what might it be . . .?'

'Well, I do recall that thou did speak of Lady Avril *letting stuff in* here. Surely if things can be let *in*, then they may also be let *out*? My humble suggestion is that we search for some hidden exit. I am sure that one must exist.'

'Brilliant!' Augustus was surprised. 'That's actually brilliant, Bony.'

'Oh, Mr Dog! I know that I am but a dolt compared to thee. Thou art the true genius.'

'Well, I can't deny that. Let's start looking then. You take one wall, I'll take the other.'

Groping their way through the darkness, the two clones began to inspect the walls with their hands and paws. The room was even bigger than Augustus had thought, and the walls felt very cold to the touch. In fact, they were getting colder as they made their way slowly round the room. The air was getting even colder too.

'Mr Dog!' Bonaparte shrieked as he reached the end of the room. 'I have found an opening!'

Augustus bounded over. Sure enough, it was some sort of grille. He rattled at it with his paws.

'Help me out here, Bony. Your fingers are just the right size for this. We need to pull this thing off.'

Bonaparte wrapped his spindly fingers through the bars of the grille. Augustus grabbed his jacket with his teeth.

'Eee, oh-ar, eee!' he said.

'Mr Dog! Speakest thou in tongues?'

Augustus unclenched his teeth. 'I *said*, heave, Bonaparte! Heave!'

He bit down on the jacket again, and the two of them pulled as hard as they could. With a loud wrenching sound, the grille came slightly loose. Then, with a rather pitiful squeak, it came off altogether. The clones tumbled to the floor.

'Do excuse me, Mr Dog!' Bonaparte scrambled to his feet. 'I did not mean to sit on thy paw.'

'You didn't sit on my paw, Bony. Now, let's see what's behind that grille.' He moved towards it. The air was very cold. 'It must be an exit.' He moved closer and peered out. 'Honestly, Bony,' he snapped, as he tripped over something underneath his left paws. 'Move your big feet.'

''Twas not my foot, Mr Dog.' Bonaparte's voice came from the right.

The bolt that hit Augustus at this moment was not so much from the blue as from the depths of horror. He realised what he had tripped on. It must be one of Room 237's previous victims.

'Bony –' his voice was very small – 'I think we should get out of here as fast as we can.'

He scrambled through the space and found himself inside a small metal compartment. There was a hole about the size of a small coin in the back. He tapped at the metal. It felt very thin, and was slotted into narrow grooves, without the need for screws.

'I think we can break through this. I'm going to put my paws against the sides and you reach through and push me. Hard as you can!'

The smooth metal was as wafer-thin as he had suspected and, once dislodged from its grooves, had nothing to keep it in place. In fact, if he had known just how easily it was going to come loose, Augustus would not have asked Bonaparte to push so hard.

'Yoooowwww!'

He shot out into the night and landed rather painfully on his bottom.

'I am coming too, Mr Dog!' A moment later, Bonaparte had clambered through to join him.

'Right.' Augustus sprang to his feet. 'We've got to get out of here!'

'And rescue Miss Eddy, surely,' Bonaparte said. He was already shivering with the cold.

Augustus checked himself. 'Er . . . yes. Of course. That's what I meant.' He peered around the side of the building. The white van had already gone. 'But how? Avril's driven her off in the van, and it's too dark to see the tyre tracks.'

'Canst thou not utilise thy canine powers of hearing and smell?'

'What on earth are you talking about?'

'Surely a powerful olfactory and auditory prowess is common to all dogs. Indeed, thou didst exhibit it thyself only moments ago.'

'*All* dogs? Don't be ridiculous, Bony.' But Augustus was looking interested. 'Any such skill that I have is no doubt a special gift, bestowed upon me by my great ancestors.'

Bonaparte looked impressed. 'No doubt, Mr Dog.'

Augustus sniffed deeply. 'Yes . . . yes, I *can* smell something familiar . . . This is incredible . . . I'm a marvel, really I am.' Still sniffing, he pointed a paw past the building and through the thick trees. 'They went this way. Let's go.'

The bright winter moonlight was bouncing off Avril II's bald head as she drove the van through the woods. Eddy fastened her seat belt and shivered. Her hair was still damp from her interrupted and icy shower, and the uncomfortable little gown that she had been given to wear was not very warm.

'Where are we going, Avril?' she asked.

'I told you,' Avril II said. 'We're going to meet someone.'

'Who?'

'Just a friend.'

'Why didn't Augustus and Bonaparte want to come?' Avril had sworn the two were not interested in meeting anyone and had simply gone to bed. 'It's not like them.'

'For the love of Euripides.' Avril II turned and gave Eddy the sort of look that could freeze a Geiger counter. 'Stop . . . these . . . questions. It's of no concern to you.' She moved up a gear and stamped on the accelerator.

'But it *is* of concern to me. Look, Avril, you're behaving very strangely. In fact, I'm quite frightened of you!' Eddy gave a short laugh, hoping that Avril would join in. She didn't. Eddy swallowed. 'Avril . . .'

The engine yelped loudly and simply stopped running.

'Damn and blast!'

Avril II opened the door and leapt out of the van. Then she eased herself back in, undid her seat belt, nursed her whiplash injury and sprang out again. She went round to the bonnet, opened it up, took one look, spat on it, and took a walkie-talkie from her pocket.

'Come in, control. Come in, control . . .Gideon, it's me . . . Bit of a problem with the van . . . No, I *can't* fix it . . . Yes, you'd better send someone down in another van . . . Well, if they're all busy, *you'll* have to do it, won't you? . . . We're by the Old Oak Stump . . . See you in a few minutes.'

'What's going on?' Eddy asked in a small voice.

'Look, just shut up, all right?' Avril II went round to the back of the van. She came back with a length of rope. 'Just in case you were thinking of taking a walk.'

'What are you doing?' Eddy was too shocked to resist. 'Why are you tying me up? You can't do this to me!'

Avril II narrowed her cool eyes at Eddy. Then she reached over and picked her up. 'I can do what I like, dearie.' She carried her over to the stump. 'I'm not the one who's going to be experimented on.'

'*Experimented . . .?*'

'Oh, stop whingeing. Anyway, it'll all be perfectly painless.' She sniggered. 'I *think*.'

Eddy felt sick. 'Avril, I don't understand! Why would you want to hurt me?'

'Well, *Avril* almost certainly wouldn't want to.' She gave a nasty sneer. 'But I'm *not* Avril, you see. At least, not the Avril you know. Few tweaks in the DNA.'

Eddy couldn't breathe. She gazed at her captor.

'You're Avril's clone.'

* * *

'If you do not slow down, ' Dr Wetherby yelled as Avril shot past Sunny's Supermarket, 'I will report you to the police!'

They were careering out of Wretchford after Avril's short cut across the town. This had involved going the wrong way up one-way streets and several times around the mini-roundabout, backwards.

'I'll slow down when we find the clones!'

'Red light!' Dr Wetherby howled.

Avril slammed her foot down on the brake, but too late. The little green car propelled itself into the set of traffic lights, its bonnet crumpling like a paper lantern.

The two scientists were still for a moment. Avril had bashed her head on the steering wheel and was blinking to clear her vision. Dr Wetherby was feeling his face for signs of damage. Satisfied that there were none, he leapt out of the car and slammed the door.

'Brilliant!' he said, giving the collapsed bonnet a furious kick.

Avril too staggered out of the car and looked around.

'We'll have to call for help,' she said. 'Do you have a mobile phone?'

'Oh! Of course! Silly me!' Dr Wetherby patted his empty pockets theatrically. 'I must have forgotten *all* about my mobile phone when I was being *held prisoner and threatened with horrible violence!*'

Avril kept her dignity. 'Well, we'd better go into a house and ask to use the phone. We can call a taxi to take us to Leviticus.'

'A *taxi*?' Dr Wetherby was purple-faced. 'We can't leave the scene of an accident! It's against the law. No – we're calling the police! And when they get here, we'll report Blut and his bunch of criminals. These things should go through the proper channels, Dr Crump, and if you think I'm going to continue on this vigilante crusade after you've nearly killed us both . . .'

'We can't report Gideon until we've rescued the clones!' Avril spoke firmly, despite the bang on her head. 'As soon as they're safe, and hidden away, we'll tell the police everything we know about Gargoyle Manor. I promise we'll do it the right way.' She looked him in the eye. 'You have my word, Raymond.'

Dr Wetherby blinked. He was just about to point out that nobody would get up to let them in at this time of night anyway when he saw a light in a window down the nearest side street.

'Oh, go and call your blasted taxi then,' he said. 'And get a move on.'

As they got closer to the lighted window, a sign became visible above it.

'Bed and Breakfast,' read Dr Wetherby.

'*Breakfast*,' said Avril.

She had never moved so fast, and was gasping for breath by the time she rang the doorbell.

There was no answer. She rang it again.

'Please!' she called out. 'Forget the bed, just give us the breakfast!'

'Go away.'

An upstairs window had opened and was slammed again almost immediately.

'No! Don't go! Let us in, I'm begging you!' She was desperate now. She had not eaten for hours, and there must be time for a quick bite while they waited for a taxi.

'Can't you read?'

The window opened again and a hand pointed down at a sign above the door before slamming it once more.

'*No salesmen, actors, little boys, budgerigars, amorous young couples, beards, Manchester United fans, poets, ignoramuses or coffee drinkers*,' Avril read. '*Or blithering idiots*. But I'm none of those things,' she called. 'I'm a scientist. A very hungry one. And I'm in rather a hurry! We have to use your phone! Hello up there! My name is Avril Crump, and I'm not a poet, or a . . .'

'Oh, leave it.' Dr Wetherby gave up pressing his thumb against the bell. 'He's not going to let us in, the cantankerous old . . .'

The upstairs window creaked open. A very white face peered out and looked down at them.

'*Avril?*'

17

The Plan and the Van

Lionel stared at Avril over the shining clean kitchen table.

She was, without a doubt, the most beautiful woman he had ever seen.

'I'm so pleased to see you again!' he said, for the fifth time. 'I mean, the *real* you.' What eyes! What lips! What hair! (What hair?) Then he gathered himself. 'But this is the most terrible circumstance. I just let the clones walk away with your dangerous double!'

Avril shuddered. 'I can't believe they went off with her. I can't believe they thought it was me!'

'That would be because of the *cloning*, I expect,' Dr Wetherby said. 'Am I the only one round here with a functioning brain?'

'How dare you!' Lionel sprang to his feet. 'How

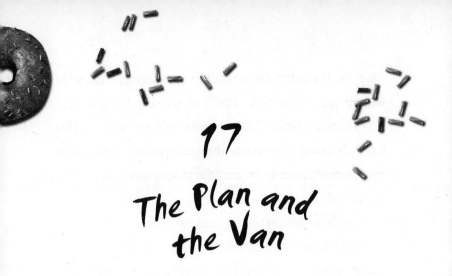

dare you insult this . . . this wonderful, *beautiful* woman . . .'

'Lionel, please. Don't make fun of me.' Avril's head drooped. The news that they were too late was almost too much to bear. The clones were gone. She could not put up with being teased as well.

'I'm not making fun! I mean it. I . . .'

Avril looked up at him in surprise. His face was blank with honesty. She felt herself turning red before remembering where she was. 'This is all my fault!' She hit herself on the head and burst into tears.

There was an awkward silence.

'Well,' said Dr Wetherby smugly, 'I can't disagree with you there.'

'That's enough!' Lionel made his hand into a fist and brandished it at Dr Wetherby. 'It's not Avril's fault! You're the one who frightened them into running away in the first place!'

Dr Wetherby did not have the good grace to look sheepish.

'Dear Avril,' Lionel continued, 'it's *not* your fault. And now –' he tried to sound as encouraging as possible – 'you're going to show Gideon just what you're made of. We're going to rescue those clones, *and* we're going to triumph over that lunatic!'

'Do you really think so?'

Lionel did not really think so. He thought Gideon sounded completely unbeatable. 'Of course!' he beamed. 'Take my word for it!'

Avril sat up and blew her nose on the tablecloth. 'Thank you,' she said. She risked a shy smile. 'It's so nice to have someone believe in me. Right.' She shook her shoulders. 'Let's concentrate. Now that my double has got the clones, they'll have been taken to . . . to Room 237. We have to find the place, and we have to find it fast. Gideon said it was in the woods. Lionel, do you have a car?'

'Well, it's a bit of an old banger really, but . . .'

'Then I'll navigate! Come on, boys. Gargoyle Manor was only five miles away, so I'm sure the woods can't be far. We'll head back the way we came.' She was already out of the door and heading for the yellow Mini parked outside.

The two men followed. Dr Wetherby, who claimed to need room for his briefcase, relegated Avril to the back seat before Lionel started the engine. They turned on to Reeke Way, passed Avril's wrecked sports car to gasps from Avril and began to drive back towards Gargoyle Manor.

'When we get to the woods, we'll find a road in and

start looking for Room 237,' Avril decided, as the houses on the edge of Wretchford began to thin out and then come to an end altogether. 'It can't be more than a few miles away. Right?'

Obligingly, Lionel turned right. There followed a great deal of apologising and three-point-turning before they were back on the main road.

'Lionel, are you *sure* you want to drive?' Avril met the old man's eyes in the rear-view mirror.

'Don't worry!' Lionel didn't want to disappoint the woman of his dreams, but the presence in his car of the most beautiful woman in the world was making his head spin. He stared very hard at the road ahead. 'I'm a very safe driver.' They lurched onwards.

'Do you always drive this safely?' Dr Wetherby groaned. He was starting to feel carsick with this idiot at the wheel. Another groan as Lionel wrenched the wheel to the left, narrowly missing a reckless rabbit.

'Please try to be nice for once, Raymond!' Avril said. 'If we're going to rescue those poor clones, we'll need all hands on deck.'

'All hands or not,' Dr Wetherby snapped, 'do you seriously think we can get them out of the clutches of that genetically modified maniac?'

'Well, if we don't,' Avril said, 'I shall blame you. It's your fault they ran away!'

'And you're the idiot who blew up the Replication Chamber and lumbered us with a talking dog!'

'Yes, but it *was* a Tor Kin Wan,' Lionel put in supportively. 'Not just any old mutt.'

'We *will* find them,' Avril said. 'We just need to formulate a plan of attack.'

Item one on Avril's plan of attack was not lurching into the centre of the road, narrowly avoiding an oncoming white van and slamming on the brakes in a frantic emergency stop. To be fair, it was probably not Lionel's preferred arrangement either. His nerves, however, had other ideas.

With an agonising screech, the Mini hurtled to a halt. The narrowly missed vehicle on the other side of the road did the same.

'You moron!' The driver bellowed out of his window.

Dr Wetherby opened his door and doubled over. The sudden swerve had made him feel really sick.

'You nearly killed me!' the man yelled.

'I do apologise, I . . .' Lionel was distracted as Dr Wetherby began to groan. '*You* talk to him, Avril.'

Avril tried to wind down her window. It stuck halfway. She opened the door and leaned out. 'I hope you're all right,' she began. But the driver was in too much of a hurry to wait around for abject apologies. He was already stamping on the accelerator and zooming away. He did not even bother to look at Avril.

Avril was very glad he had not.

It was Gideon Blut.

18
Lost and Found

'Mr Dog – might I be permitted to ask a question?'

'Sshh!' Nose to the ground, Augustus was leading the way through the dark woods. Bonaparte had trotted behind him in awed silence for nearly half an hour as the dog sniffed his way along the frozen ground. 'I need to concentrate. The scent is becoming stronger.'

'Of course, of course. I do most humbly apologise.'

Bonaparte shivered as an icy breeze cut sharply through his uniform and into his bones. By the thin moonlight, they were picking their way over gnarled and spiteful roots, and past forbidding black trunks. One particularly twisted tree loomed out of the darkness, its bare branches resembling a witch's clawing fingers. A fat and malevolent squirrel hissed at Bonaparte from the lowest branch. Bonaparte moved closer to Augustus. He was starting to feel very nervous about bringing up the rear.

Augustus suddenly raised his head, mid-sniff.

'It's very close now . . . The scent is *extremely* powerful. Eddy could do with another long shower, if you ask me.'

'Miss Eddy!' Bonaparte called out. 'Canst thou hear us? We know thou art close by!'

But there was no answer.

'Let's keep going,' Augustus sniffed. 'We can't lose her, not with my imperial nose.'

On they went, Augustus's imperial nose to the ground. The moonlight flickered on and off as they passed under patches of heavy trees. One particularly twisted tree loomed out of the darkness, its bare branches resembling a witch's clawing fingers. A fat and malevolent squirrel hissed at Bonaparte from the lowest branch.

Augustus sniffed again. 'We must be within yards of her.'

'Miss Eddy!' Bonaparte's call was tremulous.

Again, there was no answer.

'This is hopeless,' Augustus snapped. 'But my nose *can't* be wrong. I'm picking up such a strong scent.'

'Oh, Mr Dog, do not give up. Let us go on! We are so close!'

Augustus took a deep breath. 'All right.'

They carried on, groping their way through scratching briars and pushing aside hanging branches. One particularly twisted tree loomed out of the darkness, its bare branches resembling a witch's clawing fingers. A fat and malevolent squirrel hissed at Bonaparte from the lowest branch.

''Tis a most unpleasant squirrel! 'Tis thrice now that he hath hissed at me in such a vile manner!'

Augustus stopped. He turned to look at Bonaparte. '*Thrice?*'

'Indeed. A very rude creature!'

'You mean . . .' Augustus said slowly, 'that we have been going around in circles?'

Bonaparte thought hard about this. Then he smiled. 'I do believe so,' he said.

The familiar smell pervading Augustus's nostrils as he sank to the ground in despair was overpowering. And he had the sudden feeling that it might not be Eddy's scent that he had picked up.

'Bony,' he said. 'Would there be any chance that you are carrying *stew* upon your person?'

'Oh, Mr Dog, how canst thou think of eating at

such a time as this?' Bonaparte dug into his pocket. 'But if thou art desperately in need of sustenance . . .' He revealed his hand. It was filled with thick, dark, past-its-best stew. ''Tis a little cold, but I am sure 'twill taste as good as it did this morning.'

'I've been sniffing your blasted stew!' Augustus groaned. 'That's what I could smell. Not *Eddy*. A pocketful of leftover stew!'

Bonaparte was looking baffled. 'But Mr Dog, thy nose is second to none. Thy super-sensory powers are the stuff of legend. How didst thou confuse Eddy with old stew?'

Augustus suddenly wished he could drown his companion in the congealing stew. 'We'll have to start all over again,' he snapped. 'And I'll use my imperial *hearing* this time. Unless you've got any unusually talkative vegetables in your pockets that you'd like to warn me about.'

'To my knowledge,' Bonaparte said gravely, 'I am carrying no such vegetables.'

They set off once more through the thick trees.

'And if you see that squirrel again,' Augustus said, 'kindly inform me immediately.'

But after twenty weary minutes, they had not passed the hissing squirrel again. And if they had, they would hardly have known it. The wood was getting thicker and darker by the second. Pushing aside yet another shrub, Augustus's heart began to pound. He couldn't hear any distant sounds. He couldn't smell anything but stew. He did not want to admit it to Bonaparte, and he hardly dared to admit it to himself.

They were hopelessly, dangerously lost.

Avril was in a state of high agitation as Lionel followed Gideon's van at a distance over the winding road.

'Don't get too close!' she said. 'We mustn't let him see us!'

'I'm intrigued, Dr Crump. Do you actually *have* any kind of plan? Or are we just going to follow this madman until he leads us to the clones and then ask him very nicely if he'll let us have them back?'

Avril ignored Dr Wetherby and kept her eyes on the vehicle in front. It took a very sudden left turning on to a track almost completely hidden by a cluster of trees. Lionel followed.

'Lights off!' Avril said. Lionel obeyed, watching the small red tail-lights ahead intently. The way was extremely narrow, and very difficult to drive along in the pitch darkness. There were deep potholes and sudden sharp bends, none of which improved Dr

Wetherby's temper in the slightest.

'This is agony!' he groaned. 'Let's just do what I said earlier. Call the police and report Blut! Then *we* can all go home and let *them* sort this mess out.'

'I told you – not until we've got the clones back!' Avril was furious. 'They're my friends. I'm not going to let Gideon, or the police, or the Governors take them from me. And if you don't like it, you can get out now and find your own way out of these woods!' She blinked back enormous, round tears of exhaustion. Her eyes blurred for a moment and she could not see Gideon's tail-lights. She rubbed them furiously with her fists, then stared out of the windscreen again.

'*Look out!*' she suddenly screamed. For the second time in minutes, Lionel slammed on his brakes and swerved. He had seen what Avril had seen, and not a moment too soon.

'Road hog!'

Illuminated by thin moonlight, two figures lay sprawled in the middle of the track, where they had thrown themselves as the car swerved around them.

'What do you think you're playing at, driving without lights?' snarled one. 'Come on, Bony, get up. We've got to keep going.'

'But, Mr Dog, I am most dreadfully shaken,' replied the other.

Avril sprang out of the car. 'Bonaparte!' she said. 'Augustus!'

'Lady Avril! And Mr Lionel!'

'A roll call,' Dr Wetherby said. 'How useful.'

'But where's Edna?'

'*Murderer!*' Augustus hurled himself at Avril, biting and growling. 'What have you done with her? What have you done with Eddy?' The dog was too enraged to notice that Avril was not fighting back. 'And *you*,' he turned on Lionel. 'You traitor!'

'Art thou in on it too, Mr Lionel?' Bonaparte gazed at the old man in sorrow. 'Lady Avril *and* Mr Lionel – our greatest friends become our greatest enemies.'

'No, no!' Lionel said. 'You've got it all wrong! This is the *real* Avril. The other one's a clone!'

'Oh, yeah? Then what's *he* doing with you?' Augustus glowered at a smirking Dr Wetherby. 'I thought he was the bad guy.'

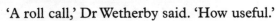

'Well, he isn't very nice.' Avril was distracted, worried by Eddy's absence. 'But he's not a really bad guy. He's just a pompous bore. I'm sorry, Raymond,' she responded to his furious splutter, 'but you know it's true.' She took a step forwards. 'I can't believe I've found you! I've been so worried . . .'

Bonaparte shrank back from her. 'Mr Dog,' he whimpered. 'Is it truly Lady Avril?'

Avril felt sick. 'It's me,' she said. 'Surely you can tell?'

Augustus eyed Avril. 'You *look* just like the other one.'

'For pity's sake! Is the concept of *cloning* completely alien to you people?' Dr Wetherby stamped back into the car and slammed the door.

'He's right,' Lionel said. 'Of course she *looks* like the evil Avril. But look beneath the surface.'

Augustus looked deep into Avril's frightened eyes. For a long moment, neither of them blinked.

'OK.' Augustus turned around and padded towards the car. 'Point taken.'

'Oh, Lady Avril!' Bonaparte's embrace as he flung himself on her was heartfelt and bone-crushingly tight. She hugged him back, as hard as she could. 'There is so much to tell thee!'

'I'm sure, Bonaparte.' Not wanting to let him go, Avril began to haul the clone to the car. 'And I want to hear every word. But we must hurry now. We've *got* to find Edna.' Now that the other two were there again, safe and sound, there was an even bigger hole where Eddy should have been. The memory of finding the little girl alive after the explosion in Lab One came rushing into Avril's head. She was praying that this time she was as lucky. 'Do you know which way she was taken?'

Augustus gestured into the darkness. Avril and Lionel waited eagerly. 'Well, it's certainly that *general* direction.' Slightly flustered, he wound down a window. 'Is it too much to expect a little air-conditioning?'

'You'll have all the air-conditioning you want, Augustus.' Lionel shut his door, started the engine and put his foot down. The icy wind blasted its way into the car. 'We've got no time to lose!'

19

The Dove and the Vulture

Gideon parked his white van between two overhanging trees. He checked his reflection in the rear-view mirror before climbing out. As handsome and flawless as ever. He smiled. Then he began to walk towards the oak stump.

'Finally!' As Avril II saw him approach, she struggled to her feet. 'I've been freezing out here!'

Gideon glowered at her. 'You disobeyed my simple instructions to bring Dr Sedukta back with you. You *idiot.* I had to send Security out to St Swithin's to find her. The state she was in, she might have given everything away. She's completely cuckoo. Keeps repeating the words "*my name is Mr Dog*" over and over again. I am dispatching her to Room 237. She is of no use to me any more. So, where is the girl?'

Avril II stepped aside. Gideon looked down at Eddy. Eddy looked up at Gideon.

'Well,' he said. 'Hello.'

Despite her fear and confusion, Eddy had been thinking very clearly for the last half hour, since Avril II had tied her up. When the mystery visitor arrived, she would talk to him, reason with him, try to persuade him to let her go. But now, as she gazed into these glacial green eyes, all coherent thought was drained out of her. She was too terrified even to speak.

'Dunno what's got into her,' Avril II yawned. 'Usually you can't shut her up.' She looked greedily at Gideon's bag. 'I don't suppose you brought any snacks, did you?'

'No.'

'Only asking.'

Gideon produced a slim torch from his pocket. He shone it into Eddy's eyes with slightly trembling hands. '*Remarkable,*' he breathed. 'To think my Mark One Replication Chamber could produce a Non-Viable like this . . .'

'Who are you?' Eddy had found a very small voice.

'I'm your creator, my dear.'

'*You're* Professor Blot?'

'Blut,' said Gideon. His lips tightened. '*Blut.*'

This was the man who had created her? The one who was going to experiment on her? 'What do you want with me?' she stammered. 'And the others?'

'Oh, the others are just waste products, my dear. Filthy mongrels. Not worth a moment of my valuable time. Not like you. Now *you* –' he shone his torch again – 'are the most . . . *interesting* specimen I've seen in some time. I'm almost proud of you,' he added, so quietly that Eddy could hardly hear him.

'I'm not a specimen!' Eddy wriggled her freezing hands and feet. 'What have you done with Augustus and Bonaparte?'

'Get my bag from the van,' Gideon ordered Avril II. 'I want to have a closer look at this.'

'Get it yourself, why don't you?' the clone grumbled.

Eddy could hardly believe Avril II was speaking to Gideon like this, as though she was not afraid of him at all. Why couldn't she just stay quiet? This sort of talk was bound to provoke a man like him, and Eddy did not want to see him get angry. She caught her breath as Gideon looked up and fixed his icy gaze on the complaining clone, but Avril II just rolled her eyes and lumbered off towards the van. 'We won't take you to the Medical Centre just yet,' he said, turning back to Eddy. His voice was very soothing. 'It's rather naughty of me, but I simply can't resist taking a few samples here and now.' He looked as if he expected Eddy to share his pleasurable anticipation.

Eddy struggled again. 'What do you mean, *samples*?' she cried. 'Let me go! You can't do this to me! I'll tell the police about this. Kidnapping is against the law, you know!'

Gideon looked genuinely puzzled. 'But I'm not breaking any law,' he said. 'You didn't think you were *human*, did you?'

'I *am* a human!' Eddy glared at him.

Gideon began to laugh.

'It's true!' Eddy said over the laughter, though her defiance was rapidly ebbing away. 'I may not be exactly normal, like other children, but I exist now, and you can't just dispose of me! Augustus and Bony too! *You're* the one who's inhuman!'

Gideon stopped laughing and looked at her for a long moment. 'A clever girl,' he murmured, 'Naturally . . .' Then he leaned very close and whispered into her ear. 'My dear, you are just a specimen for my lab, pure and simple. *Never make the mistake of thinking otherwise*.' He drew back, picked up her bound hands and began to examine them minutely. He did not look at her face again. 'And don't imagine telling the police anything. There won't be much left of you by the time we've finished in the Medical Centre. And then we'll just pop the remains in Room 237 with your friends, and no one will be any the wiser.'

'Room 237?' Eddy swallowed. 'Is that the room in the bunker? What happens there?'

Gideon did not reply. Avril II was trundling back with his black leather bag. He began to unpack it on the cold woodland floor. A small, portable microscope. A box of glass slides. A test tube. A scalpel.

'Where to begin . . .?' He picked up the scalpel. 'Just a little blood, I think,' he mused.

'You wouldn't!'

'I assure you, my dear, that I would.' Gideon was still examining the scalpel. He did not seem to want to look directly at her. 'We need information from ones like you. I am very close to eliminating all defects from my clones. As you are one of my very earliest models, your specimens will be particularly useful. I can see how far the technology has come.'

'But you can't just cut me to pieces!' Eddy pleaded. 'You made me! You can't destroy me.'

Gideon jolted slightly. 'I will do whatever is necessary,' he said. Suddenly he turned to face her again and shone the silver ring on his right hand straight into her eyes. 'Do you see this?' he said. 'The dove and the vulture. Mayan legend tells of a great flood, probably Noah's flood. After the rains had stopped, Noah sent a dove out to find dry land, the new world. The dove flew across the water until one day it did reach land. But it was starving after long months of rain, and none of its usual food was to be found. So the dove defied all the laws of Nature. It began to feast on the flesh of the drowned animals, whereupon it turned into a beautiful vulture, the ruler of the skies.' He pulled his hand away and spoke very softly. 'I am like that dove. I will challenge Nature to create my brave new world, and I will rule.' Continuing to stare into her mismatching green-and-amber eyes, he twirled the scalpel elegantly between his fingers. 'Yes,' he said, 'I think we had better begin with a little blood.' He raised the scalpel.

'Wait!'

The scalpel hovered in mid-air.

'Wait!' Eddy repeated. Hopeless though this seemed, her survival instinct was razor-sharp. 'Er . . . We've left clues all over town. If you kill me, the police will know I've disappeared, and they'll come after you . . .'

Gideon's lips curled into an almost admiring smile. 'Really a *very* intelligent specimen.'

'It's true!' Eddy yelped as the scalpel moved closer. 'The police will find out everything!'

Gideon's smooth brow, reflecting the moonlight, creased very slightly. 'I'm willing to take the risk.'

'Once you've cut me up, you won't be able to change your mind.'

'Good point,' Avril II said. She had given up all hope of getting back to the manor and was munching on a frosty twig. 'Think you should listen to her. Not so clever now, are you, Mr Perfect?'

'Quiet!' Gideon snapped, furious that his concentration had been broken. 'This will only take a couple of moments.'

'Couple of moments too many, if you ask me.' Annoyed by the lack of food, Avril II was feeling mutinous. 'It's *freezing*,' she added, slapping her arms against her sides. 'And I want *dinner*.'

'If you do not shut up,' Gideon said, 'you will *be* dinner.'

'Hey!' Avril II did not take kindly to this threat. She placed her hands on her hefty hips and stared down at Gideon through narrowed eyes. 'Watch it, pal!'

Eddy's whole body tensed. *Watch it, pal*? She could

not understand why the clone was acting with such bravado. With a man as dangerous as Blut, it seemed like complete insanity.

Gideon did not even look up. 'Be very careful how you speak to me.'

'*Careful?*' Avril II hopped gleefully up and down. 'Ooooh, you're one to talk about being careful!'

'SILENCE!' Gideon thundered. 'I am about to proceed with the draining.'

'No,' Eddy begged, squeezing her eyes shut. 'Please . . . please . . .'

'Don't you worry, dearie.' Avril II bared her teeth at Eddy in an experimental smile. 'I'll bet you a million dollars he won't do it. He's *genetically programmed* not to harm you, you see.' She scrabbled in her pocket and brought out the sheet of paper she had taken from the Document Storage room earlier, unfolding it with theatrical deliberation. 'Let's just see what we have here . . .'

Gideon dropped the scalpel and dived at Avril II before she could utter another word. They rolled across the clearing, struggling with each other like wild animals. Eddy, who was still shaking from her close brush with death, managed to crane her neck to see what was going on. The fighting pair rolled out of her eye-line and she could not crane any higher, or hear what they were hissing at each other, however hard she tried.

'Give me that!' Gideon covered Avril II's mouth with one hand and grabbed for the paper with the other. 'How dare you go through my private documents! How *dare* you!'

'Like I said –' the clone shoved his hand away – 'you should be more careful, especially with a big secret like this. What would people think if they knew you were about to dissect your *own flesh and blood*?'

Gideon clamped his hand across her mouth again. 'She's not my flesh and blood! Just because she's got some of my DNA, that doesn't make her my flesh and blood!'

The clone's reply was muffled until she managed to roll out from Gideon's grasp. 'Should have thought about that distinction fifteen years ago then, shouldn't you?' She waved the paper mockingly as Gideon tried to snatch it. '*Replication Chamber Mark One*,' she sneered. '*Experiment abandoned after accidental contamination with drop of own blood.* D'you know, I find that a bit surprising. Thought someone as vain as you would have loved the idea of a bunch of your own offspring running about the place. Or do you know something about your perfect blond, handsome DNA that I don't?'

Gideon was wild-eyed now. '*Give me that!*'

'Thing is, you should have done more than just abandon the experiment – you should have destroyed it back then. But you couldn't, could you? Once you knew your own precious DNA was in that mix, you couldn't bring yourself to harm it! No more than you can now! You can't even look her in the eye! The other two are a different matter, of course. Only have to look at them to see *they* haven't ended up with the best of your DNA. Terrible jumble, that pair. So you might be able to kill them, at a distance, but you can't bring yourself to do it with this one, can you? So don't think you can boss me around, pal! I've got your weak spot right here in my hot little . . .'

Gideon finally got his hands on the paper, ripped it down the middle, and dealt Avril II a sickening blow to the face.

'Not any more!' he spat. He ripped the paper again as the clone's head lolled. 'Not . . . any . . . more.' He stood up, smoothing down his hair and catching his breath. 'There was never any weak spot,' he continued quietly, placing his foot on her neck. 'I think you have misjudged me. I do not have a sentimental side, not even for those *creatures* whose miserable existence I am unfortunately responsible for.'

Avril II gurgled as he pressed his foot gently against her jugular. 'I'm . . .'

'Sorry? You will be. If you challenge me again, you will be. You are only here for as long as absolutely necessary and you have nearly fulfilled your purpose. I do not intend to keep another one of you disgusting mongrels alive any longer than I have to. Now, get up.' He moved his foot and kicked her with it. 'I cannot delay any longer.' He turned and strode back over to Eddy.

Avril II lay on the ground in a heap. She did not move, but she clenched a fist so tightly that her hand turned white.

Eddy stared up at Gideon as he appeared in view again, adjusting his white labcoat. He stared back at her, his green eyes unblinking and direct this time.

'Now.' He picked up the scalpel again. 'Where were we?'

20

Augustus's Imperial Ears

'I can hear something!'

Sitting in the front seat of the car, Augustus cocked his ears and held up a paw for complete silence. Lionel had stopped the car, persuaded by Bonaparte that Mr Dog's wondrous powers of hearing would locate Eddy and save the day, if not the entire world. Now Augustus put his head on one side, closed his eyes solemnly and began to rock back and forth.

'Augustus, what on earth . . .'

An opened eye and a glare were all it took to silence Avril.

'It must be some necessary ritual for Mr Dog to employ his prodigious sensory talents,' Bonaparte whispered.

Nobody breathed.

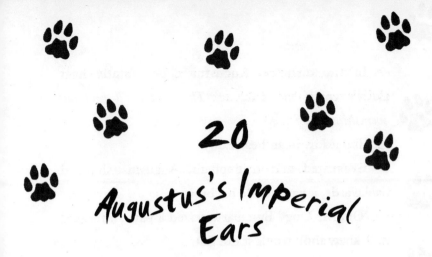

In the distance, Augustus could faintly hear Eddy's voice: '*It's true! . . . The police will find out everything . . .*'

'It's Eddy. I can hear Eddy!'

Exhausted and triumphant, Augustus slumped backwards, a paw across his brow.

'Oh, Mr Dog!' Bonaparte seized a paw and kissed it. 'I knew thou wouldst not fail.'

'Naturally. But even the greatest of us occasionally suffer the pangs of completely unnecessary self-doubt.'

'*Augustus!* Where is she?'

'It came from that direction.' He pointed towards a large clump of gnarled and ancient oak trees before leaping out of the window. Doors slammed and feet thudded as Avril, Bonaparte, Lionel and Dr Wetherby scrambled to follow him.

'What was she saying?' Avril called.

'Some of her usual rubbish.' Augustus, leading the way, was in his element. 'It's a good thing I've got these superpowers, you know. Where would you be without me? In a hole, that's where. Stuck in a great big black – aaarrghh!'

He suddenly disappeared from sight.

'Mr Dog!' Bonaparte dashed forward. 'What hast befallen thee? Hast thou been dragged into the jaws of hell by some hideous woodland ghoul? Hast thou been lured into a cruelly planted booby trap whence there can be no escape?'

'Bony, he's fallen into a small hole.' Lionel peered down into a pit.

Augustus looked back up at him. 'Help,' he spat.

'Are you all right down there?' Avril approached cautiously.

'Just fabulous. Anyone care to join me?'

'Lionel, you and Bony had better get Augustus out. Raymond and I will go and find Edna.'

'Oh, *will* we?' said Dr Wetherby.

'Like I said, Raymond, it's a long way out of these woods without a car.'

Dr Wetherby glowered at her, but he didn't speak again.

'My brave little Avril!' Lionel seized her hand.

Avril blushed. She now bore a startling, though not unappealing, resemblance to a lightly boiled beetroot. Bonaparte clasped his hands and gazed at the couple.

'A *moment* of your time . . .' An irritable paw shot out of the hole. Lionel and Bonaparte began to pull at it as Avril and Dr Wetherby hurried onwards through the oak grove.

Moving with remarkable speed, Avril thrust aside

a couple of shrubs. The voices ahead of them were getting louder.

'It's hard enough with mutant brats offering opinions left, right and centre. I will not tolerate your input as well!'

Suddenly Avril could see Eddy. She was in the middle of the clearing ahead, trussed up and hovered over by a scalpel-wielding Gideon.

'Edna!'

Quick as lightning, Dr Wetherby seized Avril's sleeve and pulled her behind a large tree trunk.

'Stop, you stupid woman!' he whispered. 'We can't just go barging in there!'

'Nonsense. There's two of us and only . . .' Avril had just seen the clone of herself. It was stamping about irritably and muttering. Unlike the rejects in the cupboard at Gargoyle Manor, it was in possession of the correct amount of limbs, but that did nothing to comfort Avril. Setting eyes on a walking, talking, living carbon copy of herself was an experience she never wanted to repeat.

'Not a pretty sight,' said Dr Wetherby.

'Raymond, this is no time for your nasty wisecracks!' Avril whispered. But Dr Wetherby's normally smug mouth was set in a tight line of distress. Avril started again. 'OK, Raymond, here's the plan. We're even. Two of us and two of them. We'll just go over and demand they give us Edna.'

'Look, *genius* . . .' Dr Wetherby said. 'We're not *even*. If we barge over there, shouting and carrying on, he'll just kill her. He's got nothing to lose. Anyway, he's armed with a scalpel, for heaven's sake. What have *we* got? I have absolutely no desire to become an endangered species.'

'Let's have a look in this briefcase of yours. Maybe there's a spare test tube we can break and use as a weapon.'

'No.' Dr Wetherby pulled his briefcase towards him. 'This is private property.'

'Oh. That's fine then. We'll look for something else.' Humming casually, Avril glanced about the forest floor. Then, catching Dr Wetherby off guard, she leapt forward and snatched the briefcase out of his hands. Before he could grab it back, she had bashed it on a nearby rock. It fell open to reveal its contents to the pale moonlight: a charred lump of wood, the shattered and useless remnants of a few test tubes and several singed plastic bags filled with powder.

It was the ruined remains of Uncle Edgar's chemistry set.

Avril gazed at the contents of the briefcase. 'What are you doing with *this*?'

'All right, all right . . .'Dr Wetherby held up his hands. 'I confiscated it from Lab One while you were talking to the clones. I thought it would impress the Governors if I actually had some evidence of your irresponsibility.'

Avril decided it was no time to argue. 'Well, it's no bad thing to have it now. Maybe we can use one of these broken tubes . . .'

'Just mix a few of your precious powders together and cause *another* explosion, why don't you?'

Avril stared at him. 'You're a genius!' She began to scrabble through the broken box. 'If I mix this . . . and maybe this . . . oh.' Her head sank in disappointment. 'We need sugar. I can't make these ones explode without sugar.' Anxiety welling up inside her, she reached for the sharpest-looking of the broken tubes and rummaged in her pockets to find a tissue to pick it up with. 'I don't know . . . We'll just have to wave this at him and shout a lot and . . .'

She stopped. Her fingers had touched something soft and squidgy inside her pocket. It felt familiar. *Very* familiar. She recognised that sensation immediately.

It was a doughnut. The plump and perfect

doughnut she had stuffed into her pocket back in Gideon's library.

She beamed up at Dr Wetherby.

'We have explosive,' she said. 'And we have sugar. Let's rock and roll.'

21

Blast from the Past

'Please!' Eddy was sobbing now. 'Please, stop! Just let me go! I won't tell anyone, I promise . . .'

Images of her short life began to flash in front of her eyes: Augustus sitting loftily on his bucket in the broom cupboard . . . Bonaparte singing his bizarre song to a captive audience . . . Avril creeping across the forest floor bearing a large doughnut . . . She blinked. This was not a memory. Avril really *was* creeping across the forest floor bearing a large doughnut.

'Gideon Blut!' Avril boomed. 'You just hold that scalpel right there.'

Gideon turned round. His face contorted with rage.

'Avril!' he snapped.

'Well, obviously . . .'

'Not *you*! I'm talking to the other one. Avril II! Get her!'

'I wouldn't if I were you,' Avril said as the clone lumbered towards her. 'This doughnut is packed with explosive. Any sudden movement and it'll blow.'

Avril II stopped in her tracks. She looked back at Gideon. 'Well?'

'It's very simple, Gideon.' Avril took a wobbling pace forward, then steadied herself as Dr Wetherby gave a warning yelp. 'Nobody needs to die. Just put down that scalpel, untie Edna and let her go.'

Gideon smiled. He looked very handsome in the icy moonlight.

'I think you have made a terrible mistake.'

'No mistake,' Avril said. 'I will do this if I have to, Gideon. There's enough explosive in here to send us all on a one-way ticket to kingdom come.'

As soon as she had spoken, she felt that she *had* made a terrible mistake.

'She won't drop it.' Avril II was eyeing the doughnut. It didn't half look tasty. She licked her lips. 'If it blows up and kills us all, it'll kill the little girl as well.'

Gideon twirled his scalpel again, tapping his silver signet ring as he did so. 'Let's quit playing Quidditch here,' he said. 'I've got some *very* important samples to take.'

'Let her go,' Avril repeated. 'You don't want me to detonate this, Gideon. Really you don't.'

Gideon looked at Avril with utter contempt. 'Go back to the hole you crawled out of, Dr Crump, and leave me to my work.' He clutched the scalpel tighter. He stared back down at Eddy, then raised it high above her head.

'NO!' Avril lunged forward in panic. The doughnut tumbled from her hands.

'Get down!' Dr Wetherby screamed.

Everybody hit the ground at precisely the same moment as the doughnut.

There was no explosion.

'Owww!' Dr Wetherby was the first to break the silence. 'I think I've broken my ankle!'

'I *knew* they were bluffing.' Avril II lumbered to her feet and waddled forward. She could contain herself no longer. In one swift movement, she had stuffed the doughnut into her mouth and swallowed it whole. Then she burped. 'Tasted a bit off.' She burped again, much louder this time. It sounded like a small car backfiring.

'This is all *very* entertaining.' Gideon was on his feet again. 'Do your job,' he told Avril II. He pointed at Avril. 'Kill her.'

The clone was not listening. She looked in rather a lot of pain and put a hand to her stomach.

'*Must* have been off,' she said. A deep, low grumbling was emanating from her middle. Then it became a rumble. It was getting louder. Her eyes locked on to Avril's. They spoke in unison.

'*It's going to blow.*'

Gideon smiled at the two horror-struck Avrils.

'If you will excuse me,' he said, 'I have somewhere else to be.'

'No!' Avril II was lurching about as the doughnut ricocheted in her stomach. 'You can't just leave me! Help me!'

Gideon looked puzzled. '*Help* you?' he said. 'I should never have created you in the first place. You've been nothing but trouble. I shall stick to pure-breeds in the future.'

The clone lurched past him and toppled to the ground in agony, legs and arms flailing. She landed directly on top of Eddy.

Avril shrieked. 'Get away from her!'

'Hey!' The shout came from the right-hand side of the clearing. 'Where's Eddy?'

Gideon swivelled around. It was Lionel, Augustus and Bonaparte, advancing in as threatening a manner as they knew how. Augustus was growling ferociously. Lionel was brandishing a wooden stick. Bonaparte was shrieking.

'What have you done with her?' Lionel roared, purple-faced. He reached for his old police identification badge, then decided it would not be all that much use in these circumstances. Instead, he raised his stick high in the air.

Gideon moved fast. He seized Avril around the neck. His scalpel glinted.

'Come one step closer,' he informed Lionel, 'and I *will* use this.'

Lionel hesitated. His stick wobbled.

'I think Dr Crump will accompany me to the van,' Gideon said pleasantly. He began to drag her backwards, his sharp eyes watching Lionel, Bonaparte and Augustus. 'I am sure that her current position means that none of you will try anything foolish?'

'Edna's over there!' Avril jerked her head backwards. '*Underneath* my clone. You have to save her!' she said. 'There's a bomb!'

The rumbling was almost deafening by now.

'Lady Avril!' Bonaparte wailed. The three of them were frozen with indecision. And then a movement across the moonlit clearing drew all their eyes towards it.

‘Don’t just stand there!’ Avril gasped at the three. ‘Save Edna!’

‘Ah, heroics in the face of certain death!’ Gideon said. He was nearly at the van. ‘Well,’ he said, ‘it will be a shame to leave all this behind. It’s been a blast.’

Avril could not understand why Lionel, Bonaparte and Augustus were simply staring. Then she heard a noise behind her.

‘Abandon me, would you?’

It was Avril II. Clutching her roaring stomach, her eyes were ablaze.

Gideon pivoted round to face her, almost losing his balance in surprise.

‘If I go –’ Avril II looked at her hated creator – ‘I’m taking you with me.’

Gideon blinked. For the first time, he looked unsure of himself. His hold on Avril slackened slightly.

Augustus seized the moment. Ears flat against his head, legs coiled, he launched himself across the clearing, barking like a dog possessed, and bit Gideon firmly on the bottom.

With a scream, Gideon let go of Avril and swiped at Augustus. Avril stumbled out of his grip and began to run towards Eddy just as Avril II grasped Gideon in a lethal bear-hug.

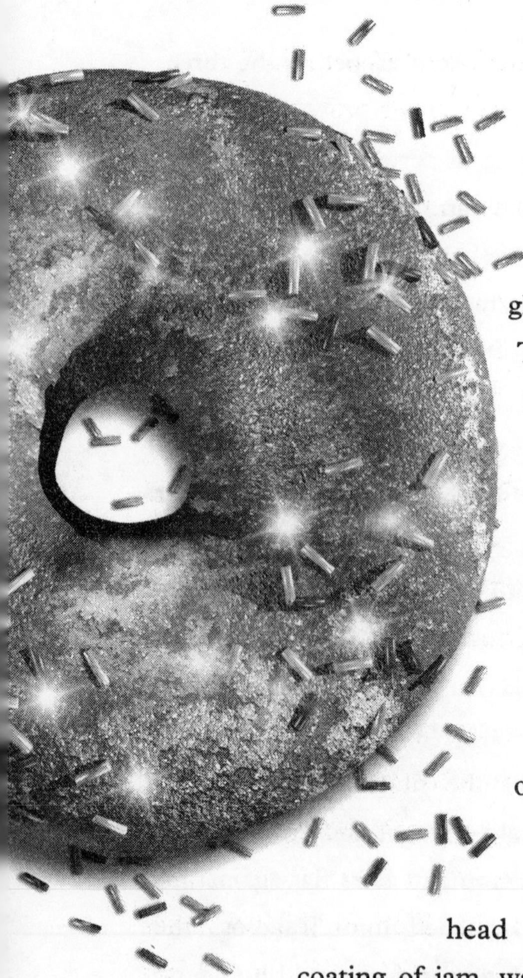

'Didn't you say it had been a blast?' she grinned.

The whites of Gideon's eyes glowed in the moonlight. There was a howl of fury.

Then an explosion.

Then a brief moment of perfect silence.

'MR DOG!'

Bonaparte, pink from head to toe with a light coating of jam, was the first to arrive at the cloud of smoke that billowed from the place where Gideon, Avril II and Augustus had been standing. He began clawing his way frantically through it. Avril, bright red from head to toe with a thick coating of jam, staggered to her feet.

'Augustus!' Her heart froze. 'Where is he?'

'He is *gone*!' Bonaparte's howls rent the ashen air. 'He is *blown away*!'

'Untie me!' Eddy called to Lionel. She held up her jam-covered hands.

Avril dropped back down to her knees and crawled into the thickest part of the smoke. She could just make out the shell of the van and a singed and tattered labcoat. But Augustus was nowhere to be seen.

'Any sign of Gideon?' Lionel asked as she backed out of the smoke.

'I can't see anything but his labcoat,' Avril said. 'Perhaps we'd better hunt around, though, just to be certain.'

'He's a goner for sure,' Lionel said. 'But that explosion will have been heard for miles around. The police could be here any minute. We just need to find Augustus and get the clones out of here.'

'We *cannot* find him, Mr Lionel!' Bonaparte was clinging to a tree, his tears streaking through the jam on his face. 'Mr Dog hath sacrificed himself to save us all. He is dead! Dead!'

Eddy cupped her hands around her mouth and shouted as loudly as she could, 'Augustus! GUS! Where are you?'

But there was no answer. Bonaparte began to sob.

'He shouldn't have done this,' Avril choked. 'He shouldn't have saved me!'

Lionel put a helpless and jammy hand on Bonaparte's shoulder. 'I . . . don't know what to say . . .'

'Edna, can you see him?' Avril ran to join the little girl, who was hacking her way through thick shrubbery. 'Is he in there?'

'No.' Eddy wiped her hand across her eyes and gave up attacking the shrubs. 'He's not anywhere. That *stupid* dog!' Eddy sniffed. 'What on earth did he have to go and kill himself for? *And* do it in such an attention-seeking way! *Honestly*, Gus.' Eddy sank into a cold, miserable, sticky heap. How one small doughnut had produced so much jam, she could not understand. 'You know how to make an exit, don't you?'

'How many times do I have to tell you?' The voice came from high above. 'My name is *not* Gus.'

''Tis Mr Dog!' Bonaparte fell to his knees. 'He speaks from heaven!'

'No, I speak from this tree. Can somebody please get me down from here?'

Four pairs of eyes gazed upwards. There, perched

perilously on a branch, a little singed about the ears, sat Augustus.

'So, do I get a reward?' He waved his tail. 'Or perhaps some sort of triumphal march is in order.'

There was a very small blob of jam on the end of his nose.

The moonlight oozed its way through the acrid smoke like a searchlight. It wove through the thick trees and across the clearing, lighting up a small ditch nearly fifty metres away from the site of the explosion. At the bottom of the ditch, there was a sudden glint of silver on an elegant hand. It was the silver of a signet ring. It was engraved with two birds.

It was moving.

22 The End of the Beginning

It was not an easy journey back to the car.

Augustus not only insisted on being carried, but also decided that being borne aloft on Lionel and Bonaparte's shoulders to the strains of "My Name is Mr Dog" was an honour befitting his heroism. Avril and Eddy were forced to help a hopping Dr Wetherby, groaning about his swollen ankle. It was a very bad-tempered and extremely sticky party that reached Lionel's car half an hour later. Only Augustus was upbeat.

'I think an extra verse or two should be added now,' he informed Bonaparte, balancing himself with a paw on the tall clone's head as he descended from his lofty position. 'This new act of bravery cannot go unmarked.'

'Indeed, Mr Dog!' Bonaparte was already taking gravy-stained sheets of paper out of his pockets. 'I shall tell the tale of thy ferocious attack on that terrible man's posterior!'

Augustus glared at him. 'Bonaparte, it *wasn't* merely an attack on his posterior. That's the sort of thing a dumb animal would do. There were many more facets to my brilliant offensive than that. Now, I want you to throw in plenty of superlatives, give a cracking description of the Glint in my Noble Eye as I plunged to my Certain Doom, and don't forget to mention how terribly handsome I am. That should do the trick.' He hopped into the front seat of the car. 'Come on, you lot. Pile in.'

It took an awful amount of squeezing and shoving to fit Avril, Bonaparte, Eddy and Dr Wetherby into the back seat, ending with Bonaparte folded almost in two across the others' laps, and Dr Wetherby almost completely suffocating Avril.

'Oh, dear,' Augustus said. 'How dreadful for you all. I *would* move, but unfortunately my terrible burns prevent me from any physical contact. And you *are* all awfully jammy.' He settled down happily.

'*I'm* the one who's injured here,' Dr Wetherby groaned as Lionel coaxed the cold engine into life. 'You've just got a few lousy sore patches on your ears.'

'Dr Nasty,' Bonaparte admonished him. 'Thou art an ungrateful fiend! We are all forever indebted to Mr Dog for his selfless bravery. He may sit wherever he doth please. Were it not for his brave assault on the evil rump of . . .'

'Bonaparte!' Augustus said. 'Just *forget* about the rump, would you?' He leaned over to Dr Wetherby. 'When he says *indebted*,' he said, 'I think he specifically means that a large cheque would compensate me for my trouble.'

'Don't be absurd!' Dr Wetherby said. 'I've never been indebted to anyone in my life. Now, Dr Crump, you and I are going straight to the police to report Blut and his horrible mob. He might be dead, but there's a whole manor-full of others to deal with. Not to mention that ghastly Sedukta woman. I bet *she's* still on the loose.'

'Actually,' said Eddy, 'I heard Professor Blut say he'd sent Dr Sedukta to Room 237. Does that mean she's . . . you know . . .?'

'Well, I say good riddance to bad rubbish,' said Augustus. 'People like her deserve to end their days in that dump.'

'No,' said Avril. She glanced over at Dr Wetherby and the two of them locked eyes. '*No one* deserves that.'

'No one but Blut himself,' said Dr Wetherby. 'And it's too late for that now.'

There was silence for a moment. Then Avril leaned over and gave Dr Wetherby an affectionate pat on the shoulder. 'Raymond, of course you and I will tell the police about Gargoyle Manor. We'll just take the clones somewhere safe, and then . . .'

'Absolutely not! This lot are going straight to the Board of Governors,' Dr Wetherby said. 'The Leviticus authorities must be informed of their existence.'

'Oh, Raymond,' Avril sighed. 'Still harping on the same old theme. Lighten up for once! No one *has* to find out about the clones, you know. And you don't even *like* the Governors.'

Dr Wetherby blinked. 'Are you mad? I can't lie to the Board. It's against every rule in the book! There is a correct procedure in these matters, and lying is *not* a part of it.'

'But Raymond, you don't have to *lie*. You just don't have to tell them. Think about it! Now that Dr Sedukta's out of the picture, we're the only other ones who know about the clones, and *we're* hardly likely to report all this to the Governors. So you're perfectly safe. In fact, it'd probably be better for your career if you *did* keep quiet.'

'Is this *blackmail*?' Dr Wetherby rooted around for his notebook. 'Blackmailing a senior scientist! That's against Rule 195 of Leviticus's Code of Conduct! You're in big trouble now, Avril Crump . . .'

'Can't somebody shut him up?' Augustus asked. 'His voice is very piercing.'

'Why don't you just button it, *dog*?' Dr Wetherby snapped. 'I've had just about enough of your big mouth!'

Horrified, Bonaparte clamped his hands over Augustus's singed ears. 'Do not listen to Dr Nasty, Mr Dog! He knows not to whom he speaks!'

'I know *exactly* to whom I speak,' said Dr Wetherby, 'and let me warn you, I'm no animal-lover! Never could stand them, and thanks to my dear departed lady wife's new career as a lion-tamer, my patience with our furry friends is just about at an end! Filthy, savage mutts, the lot of you.'

Augustus drew himself up, swatted Bonaparte's hands away with a paw, and stared down at Dr Wetherby. 'That is no way,' he said, 'to speak to Bonaparte.'

Dr Wetherby stared back at Augustus. He seemed

to have lost the ability to speak, and he was slowly turning purple.

'*Lion-tamer* . . .?' Eddy suddenly looked at Dr Wetherby. 'Do you have a son?'

'What's that got to do with anything?' Dr Wetherby snapped.

'Is his name Wilfred?' It was all starting to make sense.

'Yes, it is.' Dr Wetherby was barely paying attention. He struggled out from underneath Bonaparte and jabbed a finger at Augustus. 'Now, you just listen to me, you horrible hound . . .'

'Dr Wetherby,' Eddy said. 'You are just about the worst dad in the world. Making Wilfred do maths tests on holiday! You should be reported.'

Dr Wetherby turned round to stare at her. 'What *are* you talking about?'

'*Wilfred.* Your son! My friend! All the kids at school call him a freak, did you know that?'

'Er – no.' Dr Wetherby sounded rather squashed. 'I didn't know that.'

'No,' Eddy said. 'Too busy picking on him yourself to notice. No wonder your wife ran off to join the circus.'

'*Picking* on him? I don't pick on him. I . . . I just want him to work hard, and do well, and . . .' Dr

Wetherby stopped. His shoulders slumped. 'Bullied, you say?'

'I never knew you had a son, Raymond,' Avril said. 'Maybe he'll be happier now he's made a friend like Edna.'

An idea had just come to Eddy. She turned to Avril. 'If Wilfred's *dad* knows all about us being clones, maybe it's OK to tell Wilfred too . . .'

Avril glanced at Dr Wetherby for permission, but he was not listening. He chewed his bottom lip, which was wobbling.

'Well, I don't see why not,' she said.

Eddy's heart leapt. 'I can write him a letter explaining why we had to run away! Or maybe . . . even . . . *telephone* him.' She beamed at Dr Wetherby, suddenly filled with fondness for him. 'Can I have your address, Dr Wetherby? And your phone number?'

Dr Wetherby simply gave a loud sniffle.

'There, there, Dr Nasty.' Bonaparte patted him on the shoulder, almost forgiving him for his rudeness to Augustus.

'I never meant to make him unhappy,' Dr Wetherby said, his voice quivering. 'It's just that I think maths is so *terribly important* . . .'

'So.' Lionel drummed his hands on the steering

wheel and gazed at Avril in the rear-view mirror. 'Where to? A slap-up supper at my place?'

Avril beamed at him. 'Perfect!' she said. 'What wonderful ideas you have, Lionel.'

Lionel gulped and lurched out of the woods on to the main road. 'What a woman,' he muttered, ignoring Augustus's snigger.

Eddy looked at Avril, who was getting hot and red-faced underneath the snivelling Wetherby.

'What are we going to do now?' she asked.

Avril had been so desperate to get the clones back that she had not really thought about what she would do when she did. 'Well,' she said, 'er . . . probably we'll all sit around a table together, and Lionel will cook up something delicious, with perhaps a nice pudding for afters – jam roly-poly would be lovely – and then . . .'

Eddy smiled. 'But what are we going to do *after* that? We might be safe from Gideon now, but we're still illegal clones . . .'

'Don't you worry, young Eddy.' Lionel tried to sound as manly and capable as possible. He hoped Avril was paying attention. In fact, he was trying and hoping so hard that he stalled the engine. 'I'll take care of all that,' he babbled, as three successive attempts to start it failed. 'I've got a few tricks on hiding people.

Well, I've read books about it.' To his relief, the engine finally cooperated.

'That's something at least.' Eddy's brow furrowed. 'But where are we going to live, Avril?'

Avril felt very shy. 'Well,' she said, 'I've thought about that. Of course, you can say no. Though I think it would work out very well for everybody. Plenty of room. All cosy. But perhaps not. You won't want to. I understand. All those sponges. Not much fun for you. Still,' she finished, 'thought I'd ask. Silly me.'

'Ask *what*?'

'If you'd like to come and live with me.' Avril squirmed.

'Oh, Avril.' Eddy thought she might burst with happiness. 'Of course we want to live with you! You're our family, aren't you?'

'Yes,' said Avril. 'I think I am.'

'But it could be a problem for you having us living at your house.' Eddy was still wary of getting her hopes up. 'We're not exactly normal. And we don't want to cause any suspicion of you at Leviticus.'

'That dump.' Avril waved a dismissive and podgy hand. 'Who needs them? I'm going to do what I should have done years ago and resign. They won't even notice I've gone. They wouldn't recognise a fabulous scientific development if it blew up in their faces and turned into three wonderful clones. We'll explain this away somehow. Don't worry, Edna.' She reached over to stroke Eddy's hair and was amazed when the little girl moved to lean against her. 'Everything will be all right,' she said.

'But what about the Tor Kin Wan?' Lionel asked anxiously. 'It'll be hard to pretend he's just an ordinary dog.'

'That,' Augustus said, 'is because I am *not* an ordinary dog. I am utterly extraordinary in every way.'

'There's your answer.'

Avril grinned at Lionel. He smiled shyly back. They both turned pink.

'. . . So I think that in many ways, it all goes back to *my* childhood,' Dr Wetherby was droning. 'My parents had such high expectations of me . . .'

'Yes, yes . . .' Bonaparte clutched Avril's arm and whispered in her ear. 'Lady Avril, please assist me! I am heartily sorry for poor Dr Nasty, but I have a musical tribute to write and a triumphal stew to plan.'

Avril patted Bonaparte absent-mindedly and gazed around at the three clones: Bonaparte's eager face, Augustus's brave and triumphant (and singed) ears, and Eddy's friendly eyes. She felt that same warmth of their first meeting spreading through her again.

'. . . And I cannot think of a rhyme for posterior!' Bonaparte was sounding panic-stricken.

'*Forget about the posterior!*' Augustus bared his teeth and snatched the paper from Bonaparte's hands. 'I don't want that in my song! And you've not mentioned my looks yet. Now come on! Let's make some effort . . .'

'I'm so glad you found us.' Eddy smiled up at Avril. 'We may only be a bunch of stupid mongrels, but we really missed you.'

'Mongrels!'

Avril pounded on Lionel's shoulder.

'Turn this car around, Lionel, and drive to Gargoyle Manor!'

'What on earth . . .?'

'From the little we saw, Gideon's been conducting some very nasty experiments up at the manor.' The image of the pleading eyes and outstretched arms in the Medical Centre was still lodged in Avril's mind. She shivered. 'Who knows what other poor victims need saving?'

'But what about supper . . .?'

'Supper,' Avril announced, for the very first time in her life, 'can wait.' Her chest swelled. The blood was pumping through her veins. She could take on the world.

The car screeched around, rubber burning, and shot off through the night.

To be continued ...

'My Name Is Mr Dog'

By Bonaparte

Good friends, I prithee, gather round me
and hear my tale – it will astound thee.
'Tis but one day since Mother Earth
was blessed by heaven with my birth,
the which was so unorthodox
that, verily, 'twill blow thy socks.
Prepare to find thyselves amazed
and marvel at the issues raised
and learn enthralled, entranced, agog,
the wondrous tale of Mr Dog.

For yea, my name is Mr Dog!
Hooray, my name is Mr Dog!
All say, my name is Mr Dog!
My name is Mr Dog.

Fair Lady Avril did create
the potent brew that sealed my fate.
She travelled o'er the seven seas
to bring me talents such as these.
For Lady Avril's holy grail
were wisps of hair, a broken nail
('tis strange that no one's there to guard
leftover bits and bobs of Bard)
and in a box, she mixed the grog
that did result in Mr Dog.

For yea, my name is Mr Dog!
Hooray, my name is Mr Dog!
All say, my name is Mr Dog!
My name is Mr Dog.

But terror, danger, fear and strife
did blight my very early life.
A fiend discovered my existence
and did give chase, with great persistence,
and violent moments did ensue,
and punches hurled, and insults too!
But, glad to tell, I saved the day
in my amazing regal way,
escaping into darkened fog –
the brave, courageous Mr Dog.

For yea, my name is Mr Dog!
Hooray, my name is Mr Dog!
All say, my name is Mr Dog!
My name is Mr Dog.

So let this tale be heard by all –
the young, the old, the very small –
for such a hero's rare indeed
and rarer still when mixed of breed.
Be glad, rejoice, let praises ring,
give thanks for all the joy I bring!
The world's been made a better place
by adding to the human race
a bony man, a female sprog,
and best of all, 'tis Mr Dog.

For yea, my name is Mr Dog!
Hooray, my name is Mr Dog!
All say, my name is Mr Dog!
My name is Mr Dog.

It was I, Augustus the Dog, who selected Angela Woolfe to set down these events. She was once a student of History, and thus has some understanding of my great imperial ancestry.

Angela lives in London, a city I one day intend to rule, or where at the very least I shall light up the West End stage with my talents. This is her first novel - but not, if I keep giving her such good material, her last.

As dictated to my ~~loyal servant greatest admirer official poet~~ secretary,
Bonaparte